SO EASY TO DO

"So all I need from you now is proof of identity for our insurers, credit card, and driver's license. I already have your address, work address and phone numbers. That and of course your check."

She handed him the cards. She wrote the check.

"So how long…?"

"A week, tops. Maybe less."

"Really?"

"Quite possibly less. Could be a matter of a day or two." He smiled. "Listen. You'd better get ready to meet him or phone him or write him, Ms. Welles, however you'll want to handle it. Because I think you can consider this as good as done. Mr. Weymouth's back in your life again. To whatever extent you want him there…."

JACK KETCHUM

OLD FLAMES

LEISURE BOOKS NEW YORK CITY

A LEISURE BOOK®

June 2008

Published by

Dorchester Publishing Co., Inc.
200 Madison Avenue
New York, NY 10016

ISBN 10: 0-8439-5999-1
ISBN 13: 978-0-8439-5999-4

Visit us on the web at www.dorchesterpub.com.

Thanks to Shay Astar, Jordan Auslander,
Alan Difiore and Paula White.

OLD FLAMES

OLD FLAMES

A person who had no one would be well advised
to cobble together some passable ghost.
                    —*Cormac McCarthy*, The Road

ONE

Dora and Owen

So here I am again, she thought. *This is far too familiar.*

There was pain of course but she embraced the pain as she always did. He was big and she was not, so she could count on pain with him. Tears and sweat were pretty much the same thing anyway she thought. She was opposed to neither.

But there was yearning. That old unwanted acquaintance.

She wanted—maybe even needed this time—to see his face. A face could speak what the body didn't. His body told her he was close to coming. As was she. But that was all it told her. A glance over her shoulder was insufficient. Especially in the dark. And Owen insisted on his bedroom dark the way he insisted on taking her from behind.

But here in this room on this bed while he filled her he was emptying her too. She could feel a winding down. She fought that. Pushed back hard into his tight flat belly as though the slap of impact flesh against flesh and his own sounds, his grunts and moans and harsh breathing could meld into an invisible wind that might whirl around and enter her again through her open mouth and ears and eyes.

5

She wanted to be filled. Instead she relinquished wanting.

It was all she could do.

He woke in the dark and turned the clock toward the glow of the city lights below through the screened window. Never mind that his was a penthouse apartment. New York was never wholly dark.

He rose naked out of bed, careful not to wake her and turned and watched her roll slowly over into the space he'd left behind and nestle into what remained of his heat and thought how young and innocent she looked though she was neither and considered how to phrase his note to her.

He was still considering that when he stepped out of the shower. In the kitchen over coffee he did as best he could and then he went to work.

Owen told her once that he'd chosen the clock for the pitch and tone of its alarm as much as for its design so that when it intruded on her sleep it did so like a handshake, firm but gentle too. She turned it off and listened to the silence for a moment and knew that the apartment was empty. Owen was an early riser. She reached for the pack of cigarettes on the nightstand and lit one. Owen didn't approve but he didn't try to stop her either.

She lay back into the pillows and watched the smoke billow and drift above her. She thought that smoking was in a strange way a collaborative thing. Something human and yet not. Its trajectory could be managed by you but not completely. Its texture appeared random or somehow ordained by the mere fact of burning but a movement of the hand or a breath of air could shape it differently, turn it this way or that.

Here was proof that you existed she thought. You smoked and all at once your very breath had substance.

Who said that smoking was just a dirty habit? There was poetry.

Coffee she thought. *You're still dreaming. You need coffee.*

He'd made a fresh pot and left it on for her which she thought considerate and poured herself a cup and then opened and read the note he'd propped against the coffeemaker and though she drank what was in her cup the pot and its contents were the first to go.

The offices of Mars Black Design were at Fifth and Fifty-fourth Street. She stepped out of the cab and crossed Fifth Avenue at a yellow light which turned red half her way across. Horns blared. They could blare all they cared to. In New York City pedestrians trumped cars every time. Pedestrians wearing Armani in particular.

She signed in and nodded to the solemn young man at the security desk and took the elevator to the eleventh floor and stepped out into the immaculate stark white reception room. She noted a well-dressed middle-aged man in a plush leather chair frowning into the *Wall Street Journal* and judged him a prospective client and another much younger man whose portfolio beside him indicated a new or aspiring designer and a Federal Express messenger receiving a signature on his clipboard from Gloria at the desk—Gloria who first smiled at her and then looked alarmed.

"Dora? He's with a client. . . ."

She threw open the smoked-glass door to his office hard enough so that it rebounded off the wall and closed again behind her. She felt a moment's disappointment that it didn't shatter. He was standing behind his desk with a short fat bald man standing in front of it and he'd been showing the man some plans but it was clear that at the moment she'd driven those plans from their minds quite well.

"Just who the fuck do you think you are, Owen?" she said.

"Dora . . . this is not the time. . . ."

"Excuse me. You. Get out."

The fat man just looked at her. Nice tie, she thought.

"Dora . . . ?"

"Did you hear me? I said *get out!*"

"Another time, Owen, okay?" The man backed away.

"George . . . I'm sorry. I'll call you, okay?"

"Sure, Owen."

He closed the door quietly behind him. She pulled out the note from her purse.

"What are you? Some kind of goddamn schoolkid? A fucking *note* you leave for me? You don't even have the balls for a phone call? 'I can only hope you won't think too badly of me . . . we've not felt close for some time . . . I'll always care . .': Jesus Christ, Owen! What kind of bullshit *is* this?"

"It's the truth, Dora. . . ."

8

"Who is she, you bastard."

"There's nobody, for god's sake."

"You're a fucking liar. You couldn't tie your own god-damn shoes without a woman around to help you. 'I'll always care for you. . . .' I want to know who she is. Are you *listening to me?*"

The Qing vase on the podium beside her was a favorite of his. It dated from the late seventeenth century. Had stood on a windowsill at the Fitzwilliam Museum in Cambridge, England for forty years.

It made a loud unlovely sound against the wall.

He looked stricken. Staring at the pieces strewn across the floor. She smiled.

"You should see your apartment," she said.

"Goddammit! I'll sue you, you bitch!"

"No you won't. It'd make the papers. I'd damn well see it did."

She moved toward him around the desk. Moved in close. To his credit he stood his ground.

"I'm waiting. How well do you like your little Klee over there?"

She wondered what he was seeing in her face. Whatever it was he folded.

"Nobody," he said "Nobody you know."

And she found that while she'd expected as much, even *knew* as much, some poor sad part of her hadn't really. Had hoped that it wasn't true even up to now. Women were such fucking fools, she thought. Whoever this one was, was probably just as stupid about men as she was. She nodded.

"Nobody I know."

"Ex-wife of a client, Bill Curtis. You've never met her."

"I've met Bill, though, haven't I. How does Bill feel about this?

"I have no idea, Dora."

The rage was gone, played out. Shattered along with the vase. For a strange unsettling moment she wasn't even sure why she was here. She turned and walked to the door and stopped with her back to him. Her back was all he would get.

"You might want to ask her," she said. "If you feel like it, of course. I mean, it's all about you." She shook her head. "I haven't used this word in years. But you really do suck, Owen, you know that? In the true meaning of the word? *It means all you do is take.*"

She could hear him sigh.

"What the hell," she said. "Pretty much all of you do."

TWO

Dora

In front of the entrance to the bar they had planted a tree curbside and surrounded it with cedar chips and a low ornamental wire fence to keep the dogs at bay. Dozens of cigarette butts had turned the chips into a trash heap. She wondered why anybody would do that and poison a perfectly good tree when there was plenty of sidewalk, street and curb around. Maybe smoking was just a dirty habit after all. Or maybe smokers were just as mean as the next guy.

Hers went into the sand-filled concrete urn by the door.

The bar was the adjunct to an upscale East Side restaurant. It was dimly lit and the wood was mahogany. All they played was piano music and they kept it low which was perfect for her mood. Her workday had not been the distraction she'd hoped for.

It was not yet five o'clock so she had a choice of seats at the bar and took one at the far right corner away from the window and the barman in white starched shirt and bow tie smiled and said good evening ma'am and asked what could he get her. She told him an apple martini and watched him while he mixed and shook and poured it for her into a frosted glass all the way to the rim. She reached for it with a steady hand and sipped.

It was aromatic, cold, delicious.

By the time she finished that one and another the seats at the bar were filled and so were the dozen or so tables and the noise level had risen to the point where she could barely hear the music. Her limit was two normally but this time she decided to push it. As her martini appeared so did a young man standing to her left. He wore wide suspenders and an expensive tailored shirt and power tie and was in all possibility fifteen years her junior. A not quite so nerdy Larry King in his twenties.

"Hi," he said.

She looked at him and what she saw was cocky and grinning and holding a bottle of New Belgium Sunshine Wheat beer.

"Oh for god's sake," she said. She sipped her drink.

"Hey. What? What'd I do?"

She could think of nothing to say to that so she said nothing and then she heard her name.

"Dora? Dora Welles?"

She turned and saw a woman moving toward her past the yuppie in the power tie who decided to move on to territories a bit less fraught with nettles. The woman was about her own age and smiling and very accessorized but tastefully so, a bit overweight, holding what appeared to be a manhattan. It took Dora a moment to recognize her but when she did she gasped and got off her barstool and hugged her.

"I can't believe it," she said. "Estha! You look . . ."

"Me? Look at you! *You* look wonderful! This is amazing. My god it's been, what?"

"Twenty-odd years?"

"Twenty-five but hey, who's counting. What are you *doing* here?"

"Drinking, same as you. I live here. Here in the City I mean. You?"

"Maine. Portland. I'm just in for a sales conference. My god. Dora."

"Estha."

They laughed and hugged again. They hadn't been all that close in high school but Dora had always liked her. They had intelligence in common which in that school was rare enough but had moved in largely different circles. Dora was all visual arts and literature and Estha was math and science. And now, apparently, sales. Computers and electronics. She finished her manhattan and ordered another while Dora nursed her martini. Dora told her they had sales in common.

"I run an antique store over here on Madison," she said.

"Madison. Pricey, yes?"

"Oh yes. Pricey indeed."

"Ever get up to Maine?"

"Every now and then. I travel a lot to estate sales. I have a partner who runs things while I'm away."

"You have to call me next time. Will you?"

"Sure. Of course I will."

"You promise?"

"I promise."

13

"You married?"

"I was. About a thousand years ago. Don't remind me."

"Me too. Mine left me up to my ears in debt."

"I was a little luckier than that."

In fact it was the settlement from Sam that had opened and paid the first two years' rent on the store.

"So get this. First mine leaves me, then he goes and buys a condo in Honolulu with some little pineapple princess from Maui and they're all set up on the beach selling hermit-crab jewelry to the tourist trade. Who the hell would want to buy one I don't know. Can you imagine having this awful little spidery *bug*-thing crawling over your boobs while you're eating roast pig at some fucking luau? Got any kids?

"No."

"Me neither, thank god. Ohmygod you missed the *party!*"

"What party?"

"The reunion! Didn't anybody phone you?"

"I've been kind of out of touch. We had a reunion? What reunion?"

"Twenty-fifth, silly. Just a couple months ago. Oh god, you should have been there. Let's see . . . Laura Winger was there, Jimmy Baron, Arnie Hill, Daniella whatsername, Lydia Pincus . . ."

"Nichols. Daniella Nichols."

"Right. I've got to tell you. We girls looked a whole lot better than the men did. I mean, all their *hair* had shifted. Half of them bald as hell with funny little beards and mustaches so that you couldn't even recognize them. Anyway, *everybody* was there. A really terrific turnout. It was amazing."

"How about . . ."

"Jim Weybourne. No. He was one of the no-shows. Sorry."

She was surprised by the real regret in Estha's voice. Though probably she shouldn't have been. Everybody in her class back then knew that Dora and Jim were quite the item. For a while, inseparable. And everybody back then seemed to be rooting for them, pretty much expected them to marry. She'd been much too young to marry. And of course there was the other thing.

Estha brightened.

"*My* guy was a no-show too. Remember Ralphie Begleiter?"

"Sure I do. Second in the class, wasn't he?"

"Third. Well, have I got a story for *you*."

Estha glanced over her shoulder and as if on cue just such a balding and bewhiskered man as she'd described was making his way toward them through the crowd at the bar. He was smiling and bearish with a good dark suit and just a hint of a paunch. He was also beaming at them.

"Hey, Dora."

"I'll be goddamned. Ralphie!"

"I go out for a smoke and look what I find when I get back. Hey, come here. Gimme a hug."

His hug was bearish too. After the day she'd had it felt close to wonderful.

"How you doin'? You look . . . sensational."

15

"Thank you. I'm fine. But I . . ."

"I know," Estha said. "You're confused. He wasn't at the reunion, right? Exactly. So what the hell, I just went out and *found* him!"

The bartender asked if she'd like another. Two was her limit. Her third was nearly gone. Sure, she said. Ralphie ordered a Bud Lite.

"I guess I just got to missing him," Estha said. "You know? All those people from the old days? So I remembered hearing about this agency, some item in the magazine section or something from ages ago. But the name stuck with me so I decided to try them out. Flame Finders. A kind of specialized branch of this big detective agency. They're right here in the City. Seven hundred fifty dollars or something and they'll find anybody, if he's findable, anywhere, all over the world."

"And I'm damn glad they did," he said.

"Listen, you should look them up!" she said. "See what old Jimmy's doing nowadays."

She leaned in out of Ralphie's earshot.

"I'll tell you something," she said. "Just between you and me. He could *never* go this long back in high school."

THREE

Dora and Will

Thank god for Barbara. She was the one with the head for figures and the knack with computers. She was at it now. Keys clicking away while Dora on the other hand fine-tuned their arrangement of Victorian silver in the aftermath of their last sale. Every time she found herself forced to sit down in front of a spreadsheet she was reminded that her algebra teacher had agreed to pass her on the sole condition that she not go on to Algebra II.

Barbara had the look of a well-put-together Park Avenue matron minus the half-dozen facelifts but her heart and mind were pure Yankee steel. She was not one of the *ladies who lunch* Sondheim wrote about. In fact she cordially despised the breed—though their money was perfectly good. That sensibility and their pride in Welles' Antiques they had in common.

She closed the case and turned the key in the lock.

"I'm out of here Barb. Hope this is worth it."

Barbara smiled but didn't even glance up from the computer.

"You always bring back something," she said.

"Yeah. Last time it was a head cold and a runny nose. Terrific for sales."

"And a seven-thousand-dollar walnut side chair. Have a good weekend. Happy hunting."

The late-night drive was all she'd hoped for. Past Hartford it was all clear sailing, hardly any traffic at all ahead or behind her, her brights on more often than not cutting through the thin mask of night. She made it in under four hours. Checked into her motel and unpacked and found herself relaxed enough for nearly dreamless sleep.

In the morning she was refreshed and ready to go.

The auction was standing room only, maybe a hundred twenty people packed into the floodlit barn but Dora had managed to snag one of the folding chairs third row center. Among the locals and private collectors she recognized a number of dealers, mostly from Boston and Connecticut, but like them she wasn't here to socialize. Only to buy.

"I got a thousand two. One thousand three?"

An auctioneer with a South Boston accent, she thought. Interesting.

At one thousand four she made her bid and then at sixteen hundred went directly to two thousand. The auctioneer gave it a beat to let the number sink in.

"I got two thousand dollars he-ah, do I hear two thousand one? Two thousand one? I got two thousand once. Two thousand twice. Sold."

She smiled at the rap of the gavel. The highboy looked sort of beat now but once her restorer got done with it, it would probably fetch them twenty grand. Between that, the 1800s trestle table and the federalist blue-painted corner cupboard she'd done just fine this evening, unproductive as the afternoon had been along the roadside stores that were either overpriced or gone to seed. She wasn't interested in any of the rest of the offerings here. It was almost nine o'clock. By the time she paid and arranged shipping it would be ten. A drink was in order.

The lounge was connected to some bright motel along the highway but the look of it was strictly rural Massachusetts. There were some 1950s-vintage Red Sox photos in dandy hand-carved frames, sports banners and old beer steins, a number of good decoys and a beautiful old barn red and black checkerboard to admire and while an apple martini was out of the question here a regular one wasn't. She had her usual two. The patrons looked to be largely middle- and lower-middle-class husbands and wives except for three twenty-something boys in plain white tee shirts with their girlfriends off to her left and a single good-looking guy with cutoff denim sleeves in his midthirties she guessed opposite her at the horseshoe bar who glanced at her a time or two over his beer.

She considered an offer on the checkerboard but decided against it. No point getting greedy. The board belonged right where it was.

She paid the bartender and finished off her drink and left a good New York City tip. Waylon and Willie admonished mamas to not let their babies grow up to be cowboys which she figured wasn't a bad idea at all as she walked out the door into the humid summer night. The lot was all pickups and economy cars with a motorcycle here and there so she found her rental Lexus LS quite easily.

Her bag was in one hand and her car keys in the other turning in the slot on the driver's side door when he hit her.

Will watched the woman slide off the barstool and walk away and thought, you're paid up, she's lovely, get out of here. He picked up his gear.

He had no idea what he'd say to her if he managed to say anything at all but it was better to be a fool sometimes than not risk being one. It seemed that when he'd looked at her across the bar she'd looked back. He guessed that was enough to go on.

The Lexus came as no surprise. She'd worn the damn Lexus right on along with her into the bar. If you were going to be a fool you might as well be the queen's fool he thought, not a pauper's.

He slammed into her ribs right below the shoulder and that and hitting the car drove the air out of her lungs and sent her down to her knees on the tarmac. She was barely even aware that her purse was gone and then she was and she looked up at him running away across the lot, one of the kids from the bar and kid or no kid she was going after him the little bastard.

She flung herself into the Lexus and heard his motorcycle rev off to her right and turned the key in the ignition and threw the car in gear and stomped on the gas and then threw on her headlights. He was about to pull out of the lot waiting for a slow-moving pickup to exit ahead of him when she caught him in her lights. Her purse swung from the handlebars. She reached into the glove compartment and found the .22 pistol and held it in her lap.

He glanced over his shoulder and saw her coming up on him and she guessed he thought fuck this and instead of waiting for the pickup turned left and revved it and went over the curb instead into the street. She did the same except his landing was wobbly while the Lexus' wasn't. She slammed on the brakes ahead of him and it was his turn to hit the door only on the passenger side this time and she saw him roll away over the hood while the bike screeched across the street throwing sparks into the scrub along the roadside.

She got out and pulled her purse off the handlebars and walked over.

She pointed the pistol into his bloody face.

"You hurt my car," she said. "It's a rental."

He tried to move away crabwise. She clicked off the safety.

"Stay put, you little shit. You hurt my car and you hurt me and you tried to take my purse. You know I have photos in that purse? Photos I care about? I don't understand that. Why would anybody do that to somebody? You that fucking hungry? You were just drinking in a bar for chrissake."

"Please, lady . . ."

The palms of his hands were bloody too. Good.

"I think you should chew on the barrel of this gun

awhile. And think about it. About why you'd do such a thing. How about you do that for me."

The boy just shook his head. He was making these panting sounds out of his nose like it was all clogged up in there.

"Tell me you're a miserable little cocksucker."

He was definitely crying now. He moved his head to the side and stared down at the tarmac. She guessed he couldn't stand to look into that little black hole anymore. Maybe he saw his death in there.

"Tell me."

"I . . . I'm . . . I . . ."

He couldn't get it out. Poor kid. When finally he looked back at her she shrugged.

"Okay, don't tell me," she said.

And pulled the trigger.

The kid just screamed. She wondered if he could even hear it click. He collapsed onto the street. His jeans started to glisten in the streetlight.

"*I sure do hope you knew that chamber was empty,*" she heard someone say behind her and turned and there was the guy from the bar, the guy with the torn-off sleeves. Standing at a wary distance. But interested. He had a utility belt around his waist and held a shiny white hard hat.

"They're all empty," she said. "I hate guns."

He looked at her a moment and then laughed. So did she. He walked over.

"You want to call the state police on this joker?"

She shrugged. "He's the one with the damage. The rental's insured."

"Then how about a drink?"

She looked him over. He looked relaxed and slightly amused. She liked that.

"How about driving me back to the lot. I think I'm a little shaky actually."

"Sure. Then the drink?"

"Then the drink. Who are you anyway?"

"Will Banks. Pleased to meet you."

The kid on the street was sitting up now. Like he could hardly believe he was still alive.

"You," Banks said. "Get the hell out of here. I see you or your friends around here again I'll take up where the lady left off, you know what I mean?"

The kid got to his feet and limped toward his bike. Banks held open the passenger-side door for her. She liked that too. She thought that the damage to the door wasn't too bad considering. He went around to the other side and got in.

"You always carry that thing?"

"I've got a permit. My work."

She wasn't about to tell him it wasn't worth a damn thing in the state of Massachusetts.

"What are you, federal? Private detective?

"Not hardly."

"Well put it away, will you? Those things make me nervous."

"Sure."

"Appreciate it."

She opened the glove compartment. "No problem."

FOUR

Will

In bed he tried to be gentle but she wasn't having gentle. She rode him until he finally lurched and shuddered and then rode him some more until she did too. Then she just crumbled. He felt like his hips and solar plexus had been hit by a pair of sandbags.

"My god, lady," he said. "You do play to win, don't you."

She smiled. "You make it pretty easy."

Her expression changed. Went serious suddenly. Made him realize again that he hardly knew the woman. She reached up and moved her fingertips over his face. His cheeks, lips, his chin. He felt like he was being memorized by a blind person.

"You really do," she said.

And he was touched by this. Some deep sadness welling out of her palpable as the sweat between them. Touched and just a little shamed.

"Hey, now," he said.

"It's all right. I know you're married. There's *woman* written all over this place. And I'm going to bet you love her too."

There was nothing there to deny.

Exactly why he'd done this he didn't know. The usual reasons didn't apply. He was happy in his marriage to

Elena. The fact that Dora was attractive as hell didn't quite cut it either. But he'd known as soon as he saw her in the bar and then standing over the kid on the street that he was going to try. Guilt be damned. And he was glad he had. There was something special about this one. Something not to be missed.

"So where's she off to?"

"Her mom's. For a long weekend."

"You do this every time she goes away for a long weekend?"

"Never."

She looked at him. Touched his cheekbone again.

"I believe you."

He'd known she would. It was as though they'd been together not just a few hours but long enough so that an unspoken agreement had time to grow and pass between them. One that precluded lying altogether. She smiled again.

"So what've you got planned for the weekend?"

"Nothing."

"Really? Nothing?"

"Not a damned thing."

"So now you do, right?"

"Now I do."

He took her along his favorite path through the woods behind his house and they sat down to picnic along what he had long since come to consider his stream. She drove them in the Lexus out to Ludlow and they walked into maybe a dozen antique stores before he pled fatigue. He was not of the opinion that a lineman's job was the most fascinating in the world unless you were on the rodeo circuit maybe but she was interested so he strapped her into the body belt and safety straps and slapped a hard hat on her head and helped her hoist herself up laughing a few feet on one of the lonely poles along Sullivan Street.

They ate in restaurants where he was not known and drank in bars for businessmen.

But mostly they made love. Before Elena came home Monday he was going to have to wash the sheets and pillowcases with extreme prejudice. Fucking Dora Welles was like riding out a storm at sea on a ship upon which he was alternately captain, mate and green passenger. He could hardly get enough of it. In the lulls between he learned something of her life in New York City, nearly incomprehensible to him, about the business of antiques and about her college love affair followed by loveless marriage to someone named Wilkes who had *attempted*—and she accented the word—to abuse her. He gathered he had attempted it just once.

He told her about growing up out here in the boonies and about his father and mother and the grandfather who had raised him after their deaths by stroke and cancer respectively but steered clear of his marriage to Elena.

She asked no questions of him.

But in two short days and nights he felt that by some strange magic they had become close. He was startled to find himself a little in love with her. The slightest bit jealous of a man named Owen back in the city though she told him that was over. He realized that he wanted her to fall in love a little too. And just how selfish was that? He was a married man and she was alone. Yet by late Sunday afternoon lying in bed the storm at sea seemed largely to have passed and they rode far more gentle waves of sex. In the wake of one he asked her, was she in love? not with him of course but with anybody.

"No," she said. "I haven't loved anybody for a long time. And even then it was a cat."

"A cat?" He didn't say *you're kidding*.

"Lawrence. His name was Lawrence—after D. H. Lawrence. I was living in a four-family apartment house in L.A., I'd gone back to graduate school, it was right after I left my ridiculous marriage. But I'd had Lawrence all through that and even before, as an undergrad. He was about six years old and my best buddy. Just a mutt, a tabby. I got him at a shelter. He used to like to ride my knee. I'd be sitting in a chair watching television and if he saw I crossed my legs that was his cue, he'd jump up and drape himself lengthwise from my thigh to my kneecap and he'd watch too. He really would. And if there was music on, say a musical or the soundtrack to a movie, I'd pick him up by the forelegs and dance him along. He loved it. He'd purr like crazy. I think his favorite was SINGIN' IN THE RAIN.

"Anyhow I was asleep one night and I heard him howling. I'd had a little too much to drink or maybe a lot too much to drink—I was passed out I guess. So I had no idea how long he'd been howling. But Lawrence never howled, hardly ever used his voice at all. And he was really *loud*. So I wake up and the bedroom's completely filled with smoke. I can hardly see him and he's right down there in front of me at the foot of the bed.

"I get out of bed and he jumps down and the two of us head for the door. At least I figure we're both headed for the door. My apartment's on the second floor. And I'm all the way down to the first-floor landing when I realize Lawrence isn't with me. I turn around and there he is above me right outside my door, just standing there and smoke is pouring out of my apartment. I'm afraid to go back up so I try to coax him down but he won't come down, he just starts to howl again.

"Finally I shout at him, *Lawrence! come!* and he gets it. He trots down the stairs. I pick him up and bring him outside to the lawn, we had this fenced-in lawn, and I put him down because I know he'll be safe there and all of a sudden I'm thinking, jesus, what about the other tenants? There's nobody out here but us two. So I run upstairs though damned if I want to and start knocking on doors. Understand that I can still barely see, my eyes are tearing like crazy and I'm hacking away coughing and I'm lightheaded, dizzy as hell. But we all get out of there. We're all on the lawn when the firemen arrive and I go looking for my cat.

"I can't find him. Hell, I can't *see* to find him. I go searching across the lawn, calling him, feeling my way along the grass on my hands and knees. There's nowhere he can go but damned if I can find him. Then the emergency team starts insisting I get to the hospital.

It's an electrical fire and god knows what kind of stuff I've inhaled. I tell them I've got to find my fucking *cat* but they're scaring me about *toxic this* and *toxic that* so I finally go.

"I'm there about five hours. They're worried about my lungs, my heart, my eyesight. They even mention brain damage for godsakes! When they release me I'm half in a panic I've been there for so long, so I get a taxi home and the second floor's a drenched, burnt-out shell but the house is still standing and I go out to the lawn and I see Lawrence right away. Lying in the grass, under a shrub."

"Damn. What happened? He'd burned somehow?"

"No. There's not a mark on him. But my cat is dead. I don't get it. I'm thinking, how can he be fucking *dead?* He got me out of there. He was fine when I left him. How the hell could this happen?

"So I brought him to the vet. I paid for an autopsy. I had to know. Smoke inhalation, they told me. And he'd been gone for quite a while. I think now that probably he crawled in under that shrub and died while I was upstairs knocking on doors. There was no way of knowing exactly how long he'd been breathing in that awful shit before he managed to wake me. But if he hadn't woken me *I'd* be dead. We'd probably all be dead. Everybody in that goddamn house."

There were tears in her eyes. But she wouldn't even acknowledge them enough to wipe them away.

"Anyhow," she said, "that was my cat. I've never really loved anybody since."

He didn't know what to think or say for a few

moments. The house was so quiet he could hear the clock ticking them away.

"I'm sorry," is what he finally said. "You never got another?"

"Another cat? No. Never. Why would I?"

They smoked cigarettes and after a while made love again and smoked more cigarettes and he glanced at the clock which told him now that this was going to be the last time they lay this way side by side staring quietly up at the ceiling.

"God," she said, "New York City . . ."

"I'd like to see it sometime," he said.

Did it sound to her like it did to him? Like he was looking to be asked there? He guessed it probably did. And probably he *was* asking.

"Take your kids," she said. "When you have kids. Take them to the natural history museum and the Statue of Liberty and the zoo at Central Park. Have a drink with your wife at Tavern on the Green."

He put his arm around her and buried his face in her hair. He wanted the smell of her with him for awhile.

"You know," she said, "sometimes I'd just as soon kill a man as leave him."

He smiled. "Not me I hope."

She turned and kissed him long and deep and then she smiled too.

"Oh yes," she said. "Definitely you."

He stood in the doorway, hands in his pockets and listened to the Lexus spring to life. He watched her back up and turn and put the car into drive and then glance back at him through the windshield. He couldn't read the expression on her face in the glare of the afternoon sunlight on the safety glass but knew that his own smile was sad and he waved at her once and watched her pull away.

FIVE

Dora

She didn't bother to unpack but simply opened the suitcase on the four-poster bed and left it there. She walked into the kitchen and in the refrigerator found a carton of milk and sniffed it. Pronounced it sufficiently fresh and drank directly from the carton. Was milk lasting longer these days? It seemed it was. Was that a good thing or bad? She took the carton with her past the hutch in the hall and the bookshelves, the secretary and pie safe in the living room to the picture window which looked down from the twenty-second floor onto the lights and moving traffic along Broadway. The lights always reminded her of the lights of a suspension bridge rising up a gentle grade.

She walked back into the bedroom and set the carton down on the end table beside the bed and slipped out of her shoes and jacket. She folded the jacket neatly and draped it over the quilt at the foot of the bed. She sat down at the eighteenth-century dresser and looked at her reflection in the swing mirror. The woman who looked back at her looked tired. Driving or fucking? She decided driving. The apartment was warm and stuffy. She unbuttoned her blouse and lifted it free of her skirt and let it hang there.

Was she really going to do this? She'd thought about it pretty much all the way back from Massachusetts. Tossing out the notion only to have it creep back in again a few miles farther on. It was probably Will's fault she thought. He'd been far too good to her and far too kind.

She got up and went back into the living room to the bookshelves she'd had built years ago in Early American style, expensive enough to fool the untutored eye. She knew the book was in here somewhere. But for a few minutes it eluded her as though it didn't want to be found until finally her fingertips seemed to recognize the faux-leather binding. She pulled it off the shelf and opened it.

It opened immediately to the page she wanted, its spine broken to exactly that page. And there he was smiling up at her. A boy from decades past, fresh and clean and handsome, a boy trapped in amber. Beside the photo was a heart drawn in red ink capturing the word *ALWAYS* in printed capital letters like a cartoon balloon and beside the heart, in script, the words, *Love, Jim.*

"Jesus, Dora," she said aloud. "Good god."

She thought of what had transpired between them and how long ago and sat there awhile remembering.

SIX

Dora

The elevator had to be one of the slowest in Manhattan. When the double doors slid open she found herself facing another door with the words FLAME FINDERS— DIVISION OF THE PETERS DETECTIVE AGENCY etched in frosted glass.

The office could not have been called high rent exactly anywhere but on the Upper West Side where everything was high rent but it wasn't shabby either. The receptionist behind the desk was regulation cornfed pretty but smiled sweetly and said may I help you. I have a two o'clock appointment with Joseph Ledo she said and the girl asked her name. Dora Welles said. The girl picked up the phone and punched in his extension. I have Dora Welles to see you she said and put down the phone and smiled again. Let me take you right in.

She'd been feeling off-balance about this all along but one look at Ledo in tie and shirtsleeves conspired to unnerve her almost completely. He was shockingly young—barely twenty-five she thought—and more than a little good-looking. Rising from his computer in the small inner-office cubicle in utter comfort and assurance, smiling and extending his hand.

"Ms. Welles. Joseph Ledo. Pleased to meet you."

She shook the hand distractedly. It was impossible not to stare. Then impossible not to realize that he was *watching* her stare.

"I'm sorry . . ." she said.

"I know," he said. "You were expecting Philip Marlowe. Have a seat, will you?"

The chair was comfortable but not too comfortable. It wanted to relax you but not encourage you to stay. She watched him swivel in his own chair and pull a file from the filing cabinet behind him and then swivel back to his desk again with the efficiency of a man who'd practically worn a path to and fro. He opened the folder.

"Okay. As I said on the phone, this should be pretty much a piece of cake. Weybourne isn't that common a name and it's a man we're looking for, not a woman who may have married, changed her name and then never worked again. We know his approximate date of birth, probable place of birth, mother and father's first names, and we have a former address through what? his twentieth year approximately, though you say his parents are no longer living there. We don't have his social security number and unless you have a detective's license, the feds are tightening up on that.

"Happily we *do* have a detective's license so I should be able to find that for you too. Once I have it we can punch him up on the computer and find out all the rest. Where he lives, works, married or single or divorced, kids, phone, e-mail address, all that kind of thing. I presume you want to know all of it, right?"

"Yes."

"You figure people are about 95 percent findable, generally. Unless of course they don't want to be found. So assuming he isn't running away from child-support payments and hasn't gone mobster on you I think we're in excellent shape here."

She decided to tell him the truth. "I have to say, I don't *feel* in excellent shape here. What I feel is . . . well, I feel a bit ridiculous."

He laughed. "Sure you do. Everybody feels that way a bit when they come in. Only to be expected. It's a kind of . . . sentimental, romantic thing you're doing here. So what's wrong with that? The steely New Yorker thing is total myth. We're as sentimental and romantic as the next person. And there's plenty of room in our lives for that, isn't there? You could easily argue we don't have nearly enough of it. Believe me, you'll be totally kicked in the head when we find him for you. That I guarantee."

"If you say so."

"And I do. So all I need from you now is proof of identity for our insurers, credit card and driver's license. I already have your address, work address and phone numbers. That and of course your check."

She handed him the cards. She wrote the check.

"So how long . . . ?"

"A week, tops. Maybe less."

"Really?"

"Quite possibly less. Could be a matter of a day or two." He smiled. "Listen. You'd better get ready to meet him or phone him or write him, Ms. Welles, however you'll want to handle it. Because I think you can consider this as good as done. Mr. Weybourne's back in your life again. To whatever extent you want him there."

SEVEN

Dora

On her way home from work in the descending dusk along Columbus two things caught her eye. The first was an old woman alone and frail and tiny, no more than four and a half feet tall wearing a black dress and shawl in the manner of someone from old-world Europe who has lost a husband or a child—stopping on the sidewalk and peering into a new French bistro, not at the menu but at the decor inside, taking it in and nodding her apparent approval and then slowly moving on.

The second was a white pigeon speckled black and gray that darted out in front of her and then at her approach darted back to the curb in retreat and she thought how much she had come to like the pigeons in New York. She liked them for their beauty—if you looked closely no two feather patterns were remotely alike, all abstract minglings of gray, black, brown, white, emerald green and violet. She liked the alto thrum of their voices and the fragile sound of their wings fluttering off the ground—the same creatures she saw from her apartment window soar like eagles on the updrafts from the street. She liked their insolent bob and strut.

And she respected their resourcefulness. The long-ago cousin of the New York pigeon was the dodo—huge flightless birds so unused to man that they were hunted to extinction in just a few years for the amusement of the sailors who discovered them and who in their arrogance confounded their docile innocence with stupidity. These modern relatives were a whole other matter. Dogs chased them, kids tried to kick them, cars and cabs and bicycles and skateboards all whizzed by and while these vehicles on many occasions did plenty of harm to one another they rarely brushed a pigeon's wing. The birds lived quite well on what was dropped along the wayside or cast aside as garbage.

She thought that pigeons were wise to us beyond our understanding.

She was toweling her hair dry after the shower when she heard the key turn in the lock and the door catch on the chain.

"It's me," he said.

She digested that information.

"What do you want, Owen?"

She draped the towel over her shoulder and began to belt her bathrobe and then thought *fuck him, let him see what he's missing* and closed and unlatched the door and opened it. He looked flustered. A bit disheveled as though he'd had a hard evening and she saw that the open robe wasn't lost on him.

"Could we talk? I thought maybe we could talk."

"You want to talk?"

"Yes."

"Go ahead. Talk."

He made a stab at a grin and raised a bagged bottle of wine.

"I mean inside."

"Inside."

"Uh-huh."

She reached up to tousle her hair. The robe opened wider.

"I don't think so," she said.

"Come on, Dora. Just for a while. I've been thinking. I've been doing a lot of thinking."

"That's good, Owen. You just keep on thinking and maybe you'll have an honest-to-god thought one day. And won't that be a red-letter day for all of us."

She'd offended him. Awwww.

"Hey . . ."

She put out her hand.

"The keys, Owen. You don't need them any more."

"Dora . . ."

"Give me the keys."

"What about *my* keys?"

"You'll have to trust me. I threw them away."

"You did?"

"Yes, I did."

He put the keys in her hand. He was reluctant to do so. His eyes went to the open robe again.

"Go away, Owen. Go screw yourself. Nobody else here wants to."

She closed and double-locked the door. And the last she glimpsed of his face told her everything. The client's ex-wife had dumped him or was in the process of dumping him or he was afraid she was going to dump him. In any case there was trouble in executive paradise. She leaned against the door. She could hear his feet moving away toward the bank of elevators.

There was nothing she missed about him at all.

The phone rang so she went into the bedroom and checked the caller ID and when she saw who it was she answered it.

"We've found him, Ms. Welles," Ledo said.

"You did? My god, that was fast."

"What did I tell you."

"Tell me everything," she said.

EIGHT

Dora

The rental was another Lexus LS. She figured the last one had brought her luck. It came complete with a voice-activated DVD navigation system. So all she needed was to punch in his address and listen to a pleasant if robotic female voice now and then telling her where to turn.

What was it about bright sunlight that seemed to peel the years away? Driving up through Laurel Canyon she felt younger and stronger by the moment. As though each hill were a wave drawing her back through time. It was only when the system announced that she'd arrived at her destination—a modest white house with black shutters overlooking the valley—that she felt back in her own skin again.

Uncomfortably so. If retaining Joseph Ledo had got her to feeling slightly foolish that had receded over the four-day drive to L.A. but now in front of this house with the word WEYBOURNE on the mailbox beside their carefully tended lawn it all seemed positively insane. What had she been thinking?

The house was quiet. No signs of activity. A blue Honda Civic in the carport and room for another car behind it. She slowed and stopped for a moment and then drove on by.

She had a good dinner of steak and salad in the hotel dining room and ordered a chilled bottle of Stoli and a bucket of ice from room service and when it arrived she poured herself a stiff one and then another. In her address book she turned to the next to last page and found the name Weybourne with his own name and his wife Karen's and his childrens' Linda and James Jr. along with his street address and phone number. On a separate line she had written a Westwood address for Kaltsas, Street & Nichols, Attorneys at Law and his work number there as well.

Flame Finders had been thorough.

A few more sips of Stoli and she thought she was ready to dial. The phone rang for a while and then what she hoped would not happen, did. A bright clear female voice answered sounding slightly out of breath as though the call had found her in the middle of something. Maybe laughter she thought. The voice had laughter in it.

She found herself incapable of responding.

Hello? the voice said again. *Hellooooo out there . . . ?* This time the amusement was unmistakable.

She heard the number disconnect. She put down the receiver.

She felt like a kid caught in some idiotic prank. *Why the hell didn't you talk to her?* she thought.

But she knew why.

She poured another glass of vodka and sipped it sitting back against the pillows and after a while turned off the bedside lamp and used the remote on the TV and sat in the soundless flickering light.

The Save-on Drugs parking lot was by no means all economy cars and pickups but even in Sherman Oaks the Lexus attracted an admiring glance or two. People liked their cars here. She parked off to the right where she could see the glass doors to the National Bank of California tower across the street. According to the building's directory his office was on the eleventh floor. The penthouse. According to Joseph Ledo he would be driving a new BMW, license plate number NFB 418. Over an hour went by and she watched people come and go out of the tower and the bank and the Goodwill on one side and the Taibo Fitness Center with the SUPPORT OUR TROOPS banner on the other. She watched the entrance to the parking garage for the BMW.

There was plenty of time to ponder the tender ironies of the two signs posted as you entered the tower. One said WARNING: *THIS BUILDING CONTAINS DETECTABLE AMOUNTS OF CHEMICALS KNOWN TO THE STATE OF CALIFORNIA TO CAUSE BIRTH DEFECTS AND OTHER REPRODUCTIVE HARM*. The other said NO SMOKING.

She almost didn't recognize him at first because of the limp which made him come down heavily on the right foot and favor the left. He was carrying a leather briefcase and talking with a tall sandy-haired man with a neatly trimmed Vandyke beard whose gestures were almost theatrical. They were laughing.

They were also headed right for her. *Jaywalking in California.* Crossing the street toward the Lexus and the lot.

There was only one thing she could think to do and that was to turn her head away much as she wanted to stare at him, to take him in. Her heart was suddenly pounding. It wasn't supposed to be happening this way. He was supposed to turn left or right on Ventura or pull out of the garage in the BMW and she would follow. But here he was walking by with only two parked cars between them and he was looking in her direction talking to the other man and she had this ridiculous notion that it was possible he could recognize even the back of her head after all these years.

She didn't dare breathe until they passed. *You could disappear if you held your breath, right?* Every little kid knew that.

When she was sure they'd gone by she turned and saw them headed for the drugstore. He entered the store while the other man waited outside. She saw the man check his watch. In a little while he emerged and they walked to the corner. There was an upscale furniture store on the corner and a restaurant above it. She was guessing the restaurant. She waited twenty minutes by the clock on the dashboard and decided it was now or never.

As she walked in she saw them seated outside on the patio overlooking Ventura Boulevard. She'd been lucky. You had to pass through the patio to the left as you walked in. He and the other man were far over on the right. She sat down at the bar and ordered a dirty martini. The restaurant was nouveau Italian with both indoor and outdoor dining and she watched them having lunch outside while she glanced through the menu. There was no way she could eat. They were laughing again, clearly friends, sharing a bottle of wine. She watched him finish his salad and push back his chair and then he was headed right toward her again for the second time in half an hour and she felt frozen and trapped and emboldened all at once as he passed.

"Jim," she said.

He stopped and she could see his mind working. Jim trying to place her.

"Dora!"

She put out her hand and he took it. His touch was not what you would call electric but it wasn't unremarkable either.

"I saw you outside. I thought it was you. But I couldn't be sure."

"I've . . . gotten older!"

"You look fine."

"So do you. My god. How've you been, Dora?"

"I'm fine. It's great to see you."

"You too. This is amazing. I'm really looking at you, right? Dora Welles?"

"It's me."

"Is it still Welles?"

"Still Welles. Or actually Welles again."

"What are you doing here? Are you still in New York? No, wait. Wait a minute. Have you got a minute?"

"Sure."

"Good. Okay, let me go . . . do what I was about to do and I'll be back. Can you have a drink with me? With us?"

"Be glad to."

"Okay. Great. I'll be right back. Don't . . . don't *go* anywhere!"

The man's name was Matthew and they were associates at his law office. He and Jim finished off the bottle of wine while she nursed her second martini and looked through the photos in his wallet with more than the usual obligatory curiosity. *She's beautiful* she said and it was true. Karen was lovely—in a kind of suburban homey way. No makeup but then she didn't need any.

Want to see my springer spaniel? said Matthew.

She smiled. Attractive but too aware of it. *School clown,* she thought. *Still at it.*

On the insert opposite was a photo of the two kids grinning together poolside. Jimmy a wide-eyed skinny nine-year-old and Linda filling her bathing suit quite nicely at sixteen, her arm around her brother's shoulders. Dora was taken aback slightly. These people were real now. These people were a family.

"They're *all* beautiful," she said.

"I know," he said. "I'm the ugly gimp of the bunch."

He was far from ugly.

"How did you . . . ?"

"You know how a raccoon in a trap will try to gnaw his leg off?" said Matthew. "That office can get mean sometimes."

"Actually I blew off half my left foot with a twelve-gauge like a damn fool. My first year out here. A hunting party. One and only time I've ever been on one. You know how many bones there are in the human foot? Well I've got about half of them. None in the toes at all."

"My god."

"Trouble is, now he can only count to fifteen. Hard on a tax attorney."

Jim laughed. She managed a smile. She handed back the wallet.

"Listen, I want you to meet them. When can you come over for dinner?"

"Dinner? I don't know . . ."

"She's a hell of a cook."

"I guess anytime. Whenever's good for you. Apart from a few dealers I don't really know anybody in this town."

That was a lie of course. She'd been out here any number of times and had made quite a few friends. And none of them were dealers. She had a cousin Cassie in Westwood who liked to take her to country-western and biker bars for god sakes. She remembered a night she'd gotten so damn close to a bar fight suddenly right in front of her that she'd switched her Heineken from her left hand to her right in the event she had to hit.

"Hadn't you better check with her, though? With Karen?"

"Karen will *insist*. She's been hearing about you for what? Twenty years now?"

"She has?"

"Of course she has."

Now that, she thought, was interesting.

The last time she'd seen Jim Weybourne had been her sophomore year in college. Christmas vacation. It had all seemed fine between them then. They exchanged gifts. They made love on his bed the afternoon before she was to return to Boston. His parents were out visiting relatives and they only managed to throw themselves back together again fifteen minutes before they returned. The sense of trespass and transgression was delicious.

She'd assumed they'd be together over spring break. There was no reason to think otherwise. But they'd both been busy with exams and hadn't confirmed much of anything. So she drove to his house the day after she arrived home and his mother met her at the door. His mother seemed confused. Embarrassed. Hadn't he told her? He and some friends had flown to West Palm this year.

For his mother's sake she tried to laugh it off. Signals crossed she said.

She'd never felt so furious and humiliated in her life.

He tried calling after that dozens of times wanting to explain. Contrite messages on her phone. Spur-of-the-moment stupidity he said. They'd gotten drunk. It would never happen again, he promised. He offered to fly up for the weekend. Any weekend. She never answered and eventually the calls stopped coming.

She had wondered at the time if she would ever forgive him.

Lying in her hotel bedroom she wondered who the hell that girl was who'd been so badly hurt by him back then. If that girl still existed Dora wasn't aware of it.

She was a whole new woman now.

NINE

Dora

She'd dressed with care so as not to overstate. The early evening was turning cool. So she was not going to wilt along the way. She parked in front of the house and walked up to the porch and rang the bell.

The Karen Weybourne who greeted her at the door was a bit taller than she imagined, an inch or so over her own height and dressed in an oversized white shirt and jeans. A bit plainer and with a stronger cast to the jaw than evinced in the photo. She'd have known this was somebody's mom anywhere. A little harried, maybe, but a handsome woman radiating energy. She had a good open smile. If there was any sizing-up going on Dora wasn't detecting it yet. She thought that surprising.

"Dora! Hi."

The hand she extended was rougher than her own but the fingers were long and slim and elegant.

"Come on in. They always say pardon the mess but god! pardon the mess."

Karen led her into the living room past a staircase and into a large open kitchen, both rooms tastefully middle class, with some good pieces of Southwest furniture. Framed prints on the wall mixed with originals. She recognized a Tom Lea and a Charles M. Russell. At a quick scan, all nicely rendered. Very little evidence so far that not only a teenage girl but a nine-year-old boy were living here. She wondered where and what the mess was. *What we may have here is a perfectionist,* she thought.

"Jim should be home any minute now. Would you like a drink? Get a leg up on him? I could certainly use one. Long day, you know?"

"Thanks. Vodka if you have it."

"Tonic?"

"Tonic would be fine."

She took two tumblers out of the cabinet and put ice in the tumblers and took a bottle of Absolut out of the freezer and a bottle of tonic from the refrigerator and set them down on the low butcher-block table and poured. She was moving fast. Definitely a little wired, Dora thought.

"I love your kitchen. You could put three of mine in here."

"Apartment living, huh?"

"In New York? Yeah. Space. The final frontier."

Karen laughed. "Sit down. Make yourself at home."

She pulled out a country-style blond wooden chair and sat and Karen did the same.

"I'm sorry. I've been running a little late. Do plumbers come when you call them in New York? They sure don't here. I waited half the morning for this guy. Then Jimmy had Little League practice and I let myself get talked into a playdate with two of his friends who thoroughly trashed his room while I was oblivious down here vacuuming, running the dishwasher, whatever, so

I go up and play cop for a while, and then I find out that their mother can't come to pick them up so I've got to drive them home and . . . why am I telling you this? You don't care about any of this stuff."

"That's all right. Vent away."

"Anyway, I'm beat."

She took a long sip of the drink.

"We could do this another time if you . . ."

"No, don't be silly. I sent Jim out for Mexican. I was going to cook but . . . is that okay? Mexican?"

"That's fine."

"Good. Great. I'll cook another time, I promise. Cheers."

"Cheers. Good to meet you."

They touched glasses and looked at one another for a moment that was almost but not quite awkward.

"It's good to meet you too, Dora, finally. What in the world are you doing out here, anyway? Jim said you deal in antiques, that you've got a shop. I would've thought you'd be prowling the East Coast for that. Or France. Or England."

"There are some excellent pieces here, actually. Spanish mostly."

"You sell Spanish in Manhattan?"

She didn't sound distrustful. Though she had reason to be. There wasn't much call for Spanish in the City. But she seemed to be simply curious.

"Some," she said. "In this case I have an interested buyer."

"Listen. I've got an idea. Want to freshen these a little and take them out to the pool? Sit in what's left of the sun till Jim gets back? You can fill me in on the business. Jim and I buy some paintings now and then but not much in the way of antiques. I hardly know anything about them."

"Good idea."

"We'll need some more ice. Give me your glass."

She went back to the refrigerator.

"You swim?" she said.

"Sure. Pretty much once a week, at the gym."

"Come over for a swim some afternoon, why don't you. No crowds, no swim lanes. And I promise to keep the kids away."

"I'd like that. Thanks."

"You remember Sessions? Bill Sessions?"

"Vaguely."

They were seated over coffee. Ice cream for Linda and Jimmy. Karen had finally relaxed and the kids were nothing if not polite. Maybe a bit distant—Linda especially. But what did she know about kids these days? Especially teenage girls. Probably they were just bored.

"Sure you do. Think *way* back. Sophomore year science fair? Compared the water in all these fast-food restaurants' toilets to their melted ice and found that the ice had more bacteria in it than the water did?"

"Yecchh," said Jimmy.

"I remember now."

"I see him every now and then. Lives down in the Valley. He and Matthew—you met Matthew—went to law school together. Surprised the hell out of me. I thought for sure he'd be a microbiologist or something. But no, corporate law. Go figure. Oh, and Randy Fitch?"

"*Him* I remember."

"Right. He's in jail. Or was last I heard. Grand theft auto down in San Diego. Took a car at gunpoint and then found out it was a stick shift. And he couldn't *drive* a stick shift."

They laughed. They all did. But she had the feeling that Karen and the kids had heard that one before and that for this particular night at least they were running out of PG-rated stories and small talk. She knew she was. And Karen was plainly tired.

"It's getting late," she said. "I'd better be going."

"Not yet," he said.

"You've got work tomorrow, right? And Karen's got to be exhausted. Another time."

She stood up. They walked her to the door. Even Linda and Jimmy. Good god these kids were polite. Not like the kids she was used to seeing on the streets of New York, who were all whoop and holler and would knock you over on your ass if you weren't careful.

"Thanks, Karen," she said.

"My pleasure."

"When do you leave, Jimmy?"

He was off to camp in Colorado for the summer. Fishing and hiking and even white-water rafting. Karen said the gear was costing them a fortune.

"Three days." He grinned.

"Well you have a real good time. Nice to meet you."

"You too," said Jimmy.

"And you, Linda."

"Nice to meet you too, Dora," she said.

She shook their hands. Linda's seemed oddly warm and wet she thought, as though she'd been clenching them. Teenage nerves maybe.

"If you want that swim tomorrow," Karen said, "I'm free. After two I am anyway. I usually try to get in an hour or so around then every day if I can."

"That'd be great. I could use the exercise. Should I call . . . ?"

"Not necessary. Just come on up."

"Thanks. About two thirty maybe?"

"Sounds good."

She shook her hand and Dora was aware of those fingers again. Her own were peasant's hands by comparison. Jim took her arm and kissed her cheek.

" 'Night, Dora."

" 'Night, Jim."

In her own estimation the kiss lasted a little bit longer than it might have for a pair of old friends if only by a fraction and not at all displeased at this she glanced at Karen to gauge her but there was no reaction and only a smile.

"See you," she said.

It was a simple thing, such a small thing but late that night lying smoking in the dark that single kiss decided her or perhaps it was the memory that matched that of another kiss very much like it when they'd first met their sophomore year in high school at the Kiwanis Karnival and she and Gail on line waiting patiently for a candy apple were being harassed in their stupid schoolboy way by three older fat boys behind them, comments between them about her ass and tits in a kind of pseudo sotto voce just begging to be heard, when this fourth boy standing in front of them who she knew vaguely from algebra class turned and said that's about enough, assholes.

The boys were taken aback by this because here was this kid smaller than any of them giving them lip, calling them assholes—yet there was real threat and confidence in this boy's voice while theirs was all fat-kid bravado like *oh, big man, gonna take down the three of us, huh? big man!* tumbling from their lips like overripe fruit. The boy turned to her and Gail and said what would you like, ladies? it's on me and proceeded to buy Cokes and candy apples for all three of them.

When they moved away from the stand the boys were still talking their jive and Dora turned to him and smiled and said thank you and gave him a kiss on the cheek which he returned and held just a moment longer than expected much as he had tonight. Gail giggled and gave him a peck too which was not nearly the same and Dora was his and he hers from then on.

In the morning over coffee her idea solidified into something like a plan which she knew to be a little crazy but she dialed her cousin Cassie who nevertheless was glad to hear from her and asked her an unaccustomed favor.

TEN

Karen

"She's pretty," Linda had said. "But I'm not all that crazy about her."

Karen closed the dishwasher and turned it on.

"Hand me the wineglasses, will you? And here, you can do the table."

She tossed her a sponge. "Why not?" she said.

"Why not what?"

"Why aren't you all that crazy about her?"

She was in the habit of taking her daughter seriously unless otherwise indicated.

"I dunno. Maybe she doesn't talk to kids the same way she talks to you guys."

"She doesn't have kids. She probably doesn't know many."

"I guess. But how'd all this happen, anyway? Like all of a sudden. I mean, I know she met him in a bar. What's she doing in a bar?"

"People go to bars, Lin."

"A woman all by herself?"

Like most teenage girls out here Linda traveled in packs.

"It happens." She shrugged. "She's a New Yorker."

As if *that* explained anything.

"So they were lovers, right?"

"Yup. Through most of high school and the first cou ple years of college."

"That means they slept together, right?"

"Right. They did."

"Doesn't that *bother* you?"

So that was it.

She placed the last wineglass carefully down on the drainer and wiped her hands on a dish towel and turned to her.

"Okay. Here's how it went. Your father used to care about Dora very much. They even talked about marriage when they were kids but they were way too young for that. So they went off to different colleges and your father started . . . you know . . . seeing other girls. He's in college, right? Nothing serious. But then he did something that was not very nice and that he later regretted. He stood her up during spring break their sophomore year. Instead of going home like they'd planned he went off to Lauderdale or West Palm Beach or wherever with some of his drinking buddies. He realized right off that he'd made a mistake. But Dora wouldn't talk to him after that."

"Dad did that? God, I don't blame her."

"Hey, she could have confronted him, talked about it, but basically no, I guess neither do I. But he was just a kid, Lin. They both were. And he felt a terrible amount of guilt over it for a very long time. First loves, y'know? They're rough on everybody."

Lin grunted. "Tell me about it."

"So if you ask me, does it bother me, I guess it does a

59

little because I know how hurtful this kind of thing can be. You have to feel bad for her back then. For both of them really. Because your dad paid for what he did. It was a very long time ago, though. It's not as though she's still hurting or he's still hurting. But if you mean, am I jealous that they had sex together twenty-five years ago, before your dad even met me, the answer's no. *Our* story—your dad's and mine—has a whole lot happier ending, right?"

It crossed her mind to wonder if she was being wholly honest about this. She'd noticed that kiss. She'd decided it was simple affection, easy to ignore.

"You fight sometimes."

"Sure we do. You're damn right we do. And we make up too. That's the way it's supposed to be. Now, you want to go see what they're watching out there?"

"LAW AND ORDER reruns. Wanna bet?"

Later in the night lying next to him she heard him moan and saw him turn away from her toward the window which was in no way unusual for him. She sat up and looked at him for a moment. Sleep and moonlight lifting out the boy from inside the man.

The afternoon sun was comparatively gentle and her own skin tanned and well up to it but she worried about Dora who was very fair. All she had was an SPF 5 sunscreen to offer and Dora had brought none at all so she'd used that. But Karen figured she'd best keep an eye on her.

"Poke yourself now and then, will you?" she said. "See if you're done?"

"I promise. I've had sun poisoning before. It's not something I'd like to try again."

They sat in low deck chairs by the edge of the pool sipping frozen margueritas. She realized that hers was nearly gone while Dora had barely touched hers. Was this nervous drinking? She didn't *feel* particularly nervous.

Dora sighed. "I could get used to this."

"Oh, you get used to it all right. You even get spoiled. I honestly don't know if I could handle living in a city anymore. Up here isn't Los Angeles. Los Angeles is a million miles away. Down there in all the exhaust fumes."

She hoped that didn't sound like criticism. Dora had chosen a hotel down there in the middle of town. It was an expensive hotel. When for the same money she could have chosen the Bel-Air up in the hills.

"You know you can feel free to use this any time you want, Dora. Whether we're here or not. The house is always locked but the gate to the pool never is. Not a whole lot of crime up here. They patrol like crazy."

"Thanks. I might take you up on that. You're a lucky woman, Karen."

"You think so? Hell, I always thought Jim was the lucky one."

She laughed. "That too."

"Your own life doesn't seem too shabby. No bosses. Travel. I miss travel."

"I make a good living For the most part I enjoy what I do and hell, I've always liked New York believe it or not. But I sometimes think I'd throw it all over and trade with you in a minute, you know?"

Karen looked at her. She was serious.

"Really?"

"A guy who loves you. Kids who love you. A life, clean and simple."

"Clean. Not so simple."

"You know what I mean."

She guessed she did.

"You know what I think?" she said.

"What."

"I think you need to meet a really nice guy."

"I did. Just recently. He was in love with his wife."

"One without a wife."

She took down most of her drink in one long swallow. So that now they were pretty much even.

"They all have wives," she said.

"Nah. Not all."

An idea had occurred to her. It might be a dumb idea and it might not.

"There's more in the blender. You ready?"

"Sure. But I think I'm going in."

"Okay. I'll get us the drinks and you have a swim."

They got up out of the deck chairs and Dora handed her her glass and she had a moment to admire the flat tight body of a woman who she suspected exercised more regularly and rigorously than she did and who had borne no children before Dora stood on her toes at the edge of the pool and executed a perfect dive.

ELEVEN

Matthew

I guess this wasn't the best idea Karen's ever had was it?
he'd said and she'd smiled and said *guess not, Matthew,*
because they'd spent more time at dinner awkwardly
silent than talking. His jokes had fallen flat. His charm
had fallen flat. In fact she seemed almost hostile when
he tried to turn on the good old Matthew charm. She
wasn't much interested in his life here in L.A. or talking
about her own life in New York. Only when they spoke
of Karen and Jim did she seem much interested in
what he had to say. So that he was surprised as hell
when she said, you want to come on up?

Come up and have a drink with me, she said. Maybe
we can iron out some of the rough spots. You sure? he
said and she nodded so he pulled up in front of the hotel and handed the keys to the parking valet and followed her through the lobby and up to room eight
eleven. His flop sweat had evaporated.

Inside she poured them each an Absolut on the
rocks and they sat and she crossed those long lovely
legs. Peace, she said and they drank to that though
they had never really been fighting.

He was aware of her studying him a moment and
then she said tell me something Matthew. Do you think

people have to actually like one another in order to have sex together? Do you think it's important? He wasn't a fool. It wasn't a question. She was inviting him to dance. Even if it was coming out of nowhere the woman was still as attractive as hell.

No, he said. Absolutely not. You absolutely do not have to like one another to have sex together. No way.

You like top or bottom? she said and he told her he liked both which was true enough and the next thing he knew he was fucking his best buddy's former high school girlfriend.

And the next thing he knew she was tying him to the bedposts. With silk scarves no less. And the lady knew how to tie a knot. I'm going to fuck you till you *scream*, Matthew she told him and he said sounds about right and she was pretty much as good as her word. We're not done yet she said. Tell me when you're ready.

He wasn't a kid anymore and it had been a while since he'd had two erections in a row but she took him there all right. They say asphyxia adds to the fun she said and slid herself onto his cock and pulled a pillow out from under his head and held it over his face and he didn't think it was fun at all. In fact it wasn't long before he wilted inside her completely and thrashed his arms and legs and tried with everything he had to pull free of the knotted scarves but they held and he could hear her laughing over his own muted shouts inside the pillow while she rode him like a bronco and he simply tried to fucking breathe.

He felt her lean in close. You going to yell if I quit? she said. He shook his head no. A definite no. She removed the pillow. He gasped for air. Want to try again? No! he said but she put the pillow over his head anyway and he tried to fight her again but she was much stronger than she looked and he was going crazy down there just trying to suck air into his lungs until finally she tossed the pillow off him and smiled and said, we're done now. She stroked his face. He wanted to scream at her and call her the crazy bitch she sure as hell was but he was afraid that might just get him the goddamn pillow again.

We're done now, she said. You have nothing to worry about. You just lie there awhile and compose yourself and I'm going to shower and get dressed. I know you're probably pretty mad at me right now. So what I'm going to do is go out for a little while and just before I go I'll untie one of your wrists and leave you to handle the rest. Fair enough? And please don't have any ideas about waiting around for me till I get back, okay? To have it out with me I mean? I guarantee you wouldn't win and you wouldn't like it.

He asked her why. Why the hell had she done this? You were flirting with me all through dinner she said. Quite the lover-boy.

I'm sick of that.

TWELVE

Jim and Karen

"I'm telling you she damn near killed me. The woman's a fucking lunatic!"

Jim held his cell phone in one hand and with the other removed first the mayo, then Dijon mustard and a head of lettuce from the refrigerator and handed them to Karen who was listening to his side of all this while making them toasted Virginia ham sandwiches. One for each of them and one for Linda and her friends Beth and Suzie who were sunbathing out by the pool in what he considered to be *almost* swimsuits.

He gave Karen a look and laughed and she returned the look. It was Matthew after all. Another Matthew adventure.

"I guess you did something to annoy her."

"Annoy her? We were having *sex* for chrissake!"

"Come on, Matthew. She was playing with you. So it got out of hand, right? I mean, what'd you . . ."

He shook his head. Karen rolled her eyes and slathered on the mayo.

". . . what'd you let her tie you up for in the first place?"

"I don't know! It seemed like a good idea at the time!

Jesus! Can I get a little sympathy here? She ever do that with you?"

"Tie me up? Hell no, of course not."

"Well, lucky you. I'm telling you, I'd *lose* that one if I were you. She's wacked! I mean, I don't think you're taking me too seriously here, James."

"Of course I'm taking you seriously, Matt."

They both nearly broke up at that one.

"Honestly. I am. I'll definitely take it under advisement, okay? Listen, I gotta go. I'll see you Monday. Sorry it didn't exactly work out, you know?"

"Right. Yeah. Okay. Monday."

"Take care, Matt. Bye."

Karen sliced the sandwiches and smiled at him.

"She really tied him up?"

"She sure did. Then put a pillow over his face and held it there. I don't get it. I mean, *Dora?* I knew she could be a pistol sometimes but I'd never have thought her the type, you know? Not in a million years."

"To screw on the first date?"

"No. To go in for the kinky stuff."

She handed him his sandwich and kissed him on the cheek.

"Maybe everybody's the type, Jim. Ever think of that? Right time. Right place. Right guy. Or in this case maybe, wrong guy?"

Then she turned his head in her hand and kissed him much more thoroughly.

"So nobody's ever tied you to the bedposts, huh?" she said. "Damn. That's too bad. Maybe we'll have to fix that one of these days. Call the girls, will you? Lunch is ready."

And later that night they had long since gone to bed when the phone rang again and she was listening to Jim's end of the conversation a second time.

Hello? Oh hi. No, that's okay. We just tend to turn in early, you know? Kids. It's okay, honest. Of course we can. Sure. Don't be silly. I'm free by around five. Hey. You all right? Okay. Good. G'night.

She watched him put the phone down on its stand and turn off the light and felt his familiar weight beside her.

"Your girlfriend?" she said.

"Very cute, Karen."

"She want to confess?"

"Something like that, I guess."

"I'd like to be a fly on the wall for *that* conversation."

"Ha! I'd like to have been a fly on the wall *last night.* I'll fill you in, I promise. All the gory details. All right?"

"All right. Kiss me good night."

"I already did."

"Do it again."

So he did.

In the morning as she was packing Jimmy off for his last day of school it occurred to her to wonder exactly what he'd meant by wishing he were a fly on the wall *last night* and for a single unsettling moment and since she'd already seen Dora stepping out of a pool in a tight wet swimsuit she was able to do just that.

See her naked. Leaning over a man on a bed. Her breasts and shoulders gleaming.

Pressing down on a pillow.

It was a moment she could have done without.

THIRTEEN

Jim and Dora

He was annoyed with her. Dora could see that. Though to his credit he was trying not to show it. She didn't blame him. She was annoyed with herself truth be told. What she'd done with Matthew was stupid and not in line with the rest of her thinking about this at all. She'd told herself at first that it was that damned self-satisfied smirk of his that had gotten to her finally but men had smirked at her before. It wasn't that.

It was when they were talking about Jim and Karen and he'd said oh-so-sincerely that he'd thought of settling down himself one day just like they had, he was seriously considering it—and that just fucking galled her. He was the kind of man who would never settle down. Even if he married some poor silly-ass excuse for a woman he'd have his prick in his hand for every other woman he met.

So she'd decided to prove it to him. What a hound he was. He'd even fuck Jim's ex. And then she figured it was payback time, hence the pillow.

In the clear light of day it was a mistake though. And even worse timing.

Because here she was sitting in this very nice outdoor restaurant she'd picked out for them in her summery little Ralph Lauren backless two-piece ensemble fiddling with the ice in her vodka tonic and instead of feeling confident of what was about to happen between them as she'd been the day before she was annoyed with herself and not so very confident at all.

"Dora, listen," he told her. "Matt's a very resilient guy. He'll get over it. Hell, in a couple of days he'll have forgotten all about it."

That wasn't exactly true. Matt had an ego like an eighteen-wheeler on an open highway. It was going to take him a while. In the meantime he was going to be hearing about this for days.

"*I* won't, though. I must have been drunk. I must have been *crazy.* I can't believe what you and Karen must think of me."

"We don't think *anything.* We're adults for god's sake. You were playing. So what? You're making too big a deal out of this, really you are."

Was *that* exactly true? He didn't know.

He'd noticed the guy pull into the lot in his beat-up red Chevy, half of it covered with primer and thought how out of place it was with the rest of what was in the lot and then heard the car door slam and looked up again and saw this tall California redneck with the shaved head striding toward them scanning the tables looking for somebody and then saw him focus on Dora of all people.

The guy walked over.

"Well, if it ain't Miss Lexus," he said, smiling.

His voice sounded like somewhere in the past he'd swallowed large quantities of broken pottery.

"I *thought* that was your piece of shit out there. I wasn't exactly sure, else I'd have busted a couple of fuckin' windows for you."

"Hey," he said.

"Butt out, buddy."

He put his hands on the table and leaned in close. The man reeked of sweat and threat. *What the fuck?*

"You damn near run me off the road, you know that, lady?"

"I didn't. . . ."

"*Hey,*" Jim said again and pulled back and stood up from his chair as the man grabbed her arm and hauled her to her feet and when he reached for them stiff-armed him back against the table so that he fell to his knees and heard glass shatter—her glass or his—and someone gasp in surprise to his left and then the man was leading her across the lot. He heard her shout *leave me alone!* and was up and limping after them cursing his goddamn limp and Dora resisting trying to pull out of his grasp as they crossed toward the beat-up Chevy but as he approached the man stiff-armed him again and then grabbed her head and pressed it down toward the right rear wheel.

"Smell that, you bitch? That's *brake lining!*"

And then miracle of miracles he was able to get between them and pull her free with one hand and shove the guy hard with the other.

"Hey, fuckhead! You weren't in the car with this bitch,

so I got no quarrel with you. But if you want I can damn well *make* one. You hear what I'm sayin'?"

"That's it. It's over. Leave her be. Leave her alone!"

He was amazed. The fury in his voice almost matched the guy's own.

"Fuck you. The fuck I will."

He was a big sonovabitch but the swing was high and wide thank god and he somehow got under it and then yet another miracle, pasted him a good one in the gut, a punch he could feel all the way up to his shoulder. The guy grunted and fell back against his trunk. But the guy wasn't nearly finished yet. He threw open the rear door and came out with a fucking tire iron in his fist.

Just looking at the thing scared him shitless.

Go! he yelled to Dora and he turned to follow her and felt the tire iron slam into his arm and back up near the shoulder. He didn't know which was worse— the suddenly nauseating pain or the shock of knowing the guy was actually capable of using the thing and had just proceeded to do so. The arm was going to be useless now and all he could do was pour it on as best he could heading for her car.

Which was what they did.

And he guessed the guy had had enough flesh for one day because he didn't follow though he easily could have.

Are you all right? she said and he nodded. He was fine.

He wasn't fine. He hurt like hell. When they were on the road and they were done gasping for air and the pain had diminished sufficiently to a heavy throbbing burn and he had some feeling flowing back into his arm which was both a good thing and a bad thing he was finally able to ask her . . . did you?

"No, I swear! He had the wrong goddamn Lexus for chrissake."

"Jesus. The crazy bastard. He could have killed us. He could *still* kill us if you don't slow down a bit."

"Sorry."

"We need to go back for my car," he said.

"Your car can wait. I want to have a look at where he hit you. You might need a doctor."

"I don't need a doctor."

"I want to have a look at you."

He didn't argue.

In her bathroom with his shirt off and Dora running warm water in the sink he turned to look in the mirror. The welt along his back and arm was a swollen fiery red. She pressed the wet facecloth to it which burned at first and then soothed him. She wet the cloth again.

"Lift your arm," she said.

The welt ran all the way around to his rib cage. It was gonna be a hell of a bruise. She pressed the cloth to it and pushed gently.

"That hurt?"

"Ow. Yes."

"I mean, how much?"

"I don't think he broke anything."

He was very aware suddenly of the spicy scent of

her and that he had not been this close to her for a very long time and certainly not stripped to the waist.

"That was a pretty good punch you got in, mister."

"I'll tell you. It surprised the living hell out of me."

"Me too. No offense."

She smiled and bent to the sink to wring out the face-cloth and in the mirror he could see her breasts rise and fall beneath the scoop neck of the blouse as the muscles drew them up and then relaxed, watched them rise and fall again. He wondered if her breasts were as he remembered them to be. He remembered every inch of the girl he knew then. Or at least he thought he did. This woman would be another matter.

She glanced up into the mirror and saw him looking. He met her eyes and held them steady and felt a danger fly between them noted and acknowledged by each. She didn't move, didn't straighten. Only held the facecloth cupped in her hands beneath the warm running water. He looked down to her breasts again grained with gooseflesh.

What he was feeling didn't confuse him at all though he thought it should have.

He had thought for a long time that flying to West Palm was the stupidest thing he had ever done. The biggest mistake of his life. He was now perhaps about to make the second.

She wrung out the washcloth again and now she did straighten.

She pressed the damp cloth to his back.

"I think Karen should be the one doing this," she said. Her voice was low. A hoarse whisper.

"Take off your blouse," he said. "Let me see you. I want to see if you're the way I remember you. If you're the same."

"I'm not. How could I be."

"I want to look at you."

He thought he saw fear in her eyes and something else too and then the fear was gone. She stepped back and placed the washcloth on the sink and lifted the blouse up and off over her head. It crackled with static and she wore no bra beneath the blouse but this he already knew. And her breasts were not the same of course but not so very different either—far more familiar than not and along with that familiarity came a yearning as urgent as he knew it was reckless. He held out his hand.

Come here.

He saw her hesitate.

No.

Then she took a step forward and placed her hand in his and each closed upon the other. He drew her to him slowly and slid his arms along her back and she reached up for his shoulders and he drew in the scent of her, orange and ginger, in her hair and on her skin and he pulled her close kissed her and her mouth had not changed at all.

She lit the cigarette and watched the smoke drift toward the ceiling like tiny vertical clouds in an indoor furnished sky. She felt the sweat cooling between her breasts and thighs.

"You know it can't happen again," she said. "Just this once and not ever again."

76

"I know."

His voice sounded flat and expressionless. As though he'd gone somewhere without her.

"I love you," she said. "I'll always love you. You know that?"

He didn't answer.

"I loved you all through that stupid, stupid marriage of mine. In a way I think I married Sam because of you. I think I wanted to find somebody who'd treat me as badly as I treated you. I picked Sam. Then I kept on picking them. Bad apple after bad apple."

"Hold on. You didn't treat me badly. It was the other way around."

"No? Five years we were together. Then because of one really idiot move on your part I shut you out completely. I was a bitch. Of course I was. You know I had my roommate listen to the answering machine? If it was you she had orders to erase it. I didn't even want to hear you."

"You were young, Dora. You were angry and hurt. Hell, you had a right to be."

"I grew up angry. You know about my parents. So what. Why should that be an excuse?"

He didn't seem to have an answer for that one and that was good.

"Just this once," she said and nestled closer.

FOURTEEN

Matthew

He was on his way to work stalled in traffic alongside a minimall parking lot when he glanced to his left and saw her. She was leaning rigid against her car shaking her finger in the face of a tall bald man with a black muscle shirt and biceps like grapefruits and he could see they were seriously pissed, both of them.

The guy could have eaten her for breakfast but that didn't seem to faze her one bit. The woman had balls, you had to give her that. Then he guessed she'd had her say and they both calmed down and as the light changed and traffic started to creep along ahead of him he saw her reach into her purse and pull out an envelope and hand it to him.

The guy stuffed it in his jeans' front pocket and stalked away.

And then traffic was moving again.

What the hell was that all about? he thought.

He meant to mention it to Jim but then *Freeman v. Weber* got in the way in both the morning and then later in the afternoon and at lunchtime there was Cindy from the Blue Bar who he'd met the night before smiling at him over cocktails in a way that made him think there was a very good probability of something happening there. Which their date that evening proved absolutely true.

By morning he'd forgotten all about it.

FIFTEEN

Linda

Rick dropped her off a few houses away after their tennis date because her parents weren't real fond of Rick since her brother Jimmy—who thank *god* was finally off to camp for the summer—caught them on the couch that time with her daisy dukes half unzipped and went and told their mom. She guessed Jimmy was just scared and confused with Rick's hand down there so she couldn't really blame him but it was retarded the whole big deal they made out of it. They were just basically friends with benefits. It wasn't as though they were throwing rainbow parties every weekend, it was just an afternoon couch thing.

Still though her parents had known his parents for ten years and Rick wasn't welcome in the house any more or even on the property so he dropped her a few doors down. She was walking across their new-mown lawn wondering who was parked in the driveway when the front door opened and out stepped Dora Welles in a bathing suit and open sleeveless blouse and even from a distance Linda could see she was upset.

She said hi though she really didn't care much for Dora and Dora looked at her like she was the last person she expected to see there. She slipped something into the pocket of her jeans and then she smiled and said hi.

"I'm glad I caught you, Linda," she said. "Your parents weren't home and I didn't just want to leave a note."

"They're at a barbecue over at the Finch's. Oh shit. Did I leave the door open again?"

"I guess you did. The back door by the pool."

"Ohmygod. You won't tell them, will you?"

"Course not. Listen, I've got to leave for New York. But I'll give them a call tonight to thank them for everything, all right?"

"Sure. Is everything okay?"

"Everything's fine. It's just business. I'll call tonight. Bye. See you soon I hope."

But everything wasn't fine. She could tell by her voice.

And she could swear she'd locked that door. But Rick had beautiful big brown eyes and soft hands and she might have been wrong about that.

SIXTEEN

Dora

She swung back into the lane and narrowly missed the black Mercedes that bleated down the hill behind her. She was driving way too fast for such winding streets and the tears weren't helping any either but she wanted this risk, she didn't give a flying damn. She dug into her pocket for the photo and gripped it and the wheel in her right hand while her left wiped away tears and mascara.

The photo from the box in their bedroom drawer showed all four of them in camping gear smiling into the camera. The kids in the middle and Jim and Karen on either side. All of them happy, not a care in the world. Behind them a beautiful lake in bright sunshine framed by tall stands of pine.

While she had what. Exactly what.

The photo twisted in her grip and she stomped on the accelerator and for a moment lost control and tore along a row of hedges—their branches like sudden hailstones along the side doors of the Lexus which shocked her back into some place other than where she'd been and left her thanking god that there were no sidewalks here in the hills and nobody to walk them.

*   *   *

In her bedroom the only light came from streetlights and neon shining up from the street and the tip of her cigarette. She lay in bed with the illicit ashtray beside her and the illegal pistol in her lap thinking did she dare this, did she want this bad enough and could she do it even if the answer was she did. When the cigarette was burned through she stubbed it out in the ashtray and put the pistol to her temple and pulled the trigger and then to her neck and then to her cheek and each time imagining the damage to her pulled the trigger.

It was not the first occasion she had done this and it remained a comfort to her. Why she didn't know.

As she'd told Will Banks quite truthfully the gun was never loaded.

SEVENTEEN

Dora and Karen

She drove past the house and Karen's car was gone so she pulled into the next driveway in the new gray Lexus GS she'd switched at the rental agency for the black LS and turned around. Drove back the way she came and pulled into an empty driveway two doors down across the street where she could observe traffic either way. She left the engine running. She smoked three cigarettes with the driver's-side window open and the air conditioner on high. The morning sun through the windshield was punishing despite the fact that all she wore was a little two-piece bathing suit and a light open blouse so she turned the visors down which helped about as much as Tylenol after an amputation.

Two more cigarettes and she saw Karen's blue Honda drive on past and noted that she was alone. Two more after that and she pulled out of the driveway and into theirs and parked behind the Honda. She hoisted the beach bag over her shoulder and stepped out of her car and closed the door. Which somehow recalled the image of her bags piled in the trunk as the bellhop slammed it shut a couple hours before. She'd taken only two of them. The rest she'd left in the room. She'd rented for the month.

The pool's high wooden gate was unlocked as Karen said it always was and she thought of her last visit here yesterday and wondered was it fortuitous or not that Linda had left the back door open so it was a simple matter to go into the empty house and up the stairs into their room to find the photograph. And then wondered if she had *not* found the photograph—hunted for it really—whether she would even be here.

She heard a splash and closed the gate behind her.

Karen surfaced and shook her head and ran a hand over face. Saw Dora and smiled.

"Hey, you! What happened to New York City?"

"It's still there. I just changed my mind about leaving today. Tomorrow's soon enough. I figured, one last swim, right?"

"Absolutely. Come on in."

Karen thought, take it easy on her. You could exercise all to hell and back but Dora was a smoker and swimming was all about breathing. Normally she did ten laps but Dora was falling behind after six so she figured split the difference at eight.

They clung to either side of the stair rail.

"Cigarettes . . ." Dora said.

"Quit on the flight back. In six months, come back here and make me look bad."

"We'll see. Where's Linda?"

"Taco Bell with the girls. Then a matinee of *Fog-heart*."

"Horror movies?"

"She eats 'em up. They all do."

"I wouldn't have thought that exactly her style."

"She saw *Strange Seed* six times. Go figure."

"So. What would you say to an afternoon libation?"

"Get some sun, sure. I'd say good idea."

She stepped to the first rung of the ladder and then the second and felt the familiar pull of water draining through the bottom of her bathing suit at the third rung and as her right foot came down on the concrete lip of the deck she let go of the rail and felt Dora's hands grip her left ankle and jerk her back so suddenly that as the concrete ascended she had no time for a single thought but only sensation and wonder.

"I'm sorry," Dora said.

Her voice sounded small to her and startlingly close to tears. Karen's eyes were open and blood already pooled from the wound. Her upper body was bent at the waist draped across the concrete and the top rung of the ladder. Her legs and hips bobbed in the water. Dora hauled herself up on the handrail and felt for a pulse in her neck. She couldn't tell. There might have been one. Faint.

She swam to the next ladder and climbed out of the pool and heard a car go by headed fast down out of the hills and the water dripping off her onto the concrete. She walked to Karen and squatted down beside her and put her fingers to her neck again. Had she felt a pulse she was prepared to lift the head by the hair and bring it down again to finish her but she felt none. She moved the fingers directly in front of Karen's nose. She could feel no stir of air.

Karen began to slide.

An inch first. Then two. Dora stood and watched as the weight of her lower body drew her slowly down. She saw the side of her face that lay pressed against the concrete pull up first into a grin and then a sneer and the trail of blood behind her head like a slug's trail smeared by her arms which now extended straight above her as though posed for one last dive. She heard the tiny scrape of teeth on concrete.

She watched all this in a kind of wonder.

Karen's breasts at the lip of the pool halted her descent only a moment and then her head splashed gently down to cloud the slowly stilling water like smoke from a cigarette in the lazy summer air.

She had never seen death before. Certainly never caused one. There was nothing to be done about it now so she watched. When she was through watching she dried herself off on Karen's towel and draped it over a chair to dry in the sun and then snatched up her blouse and bag and headed for the car.

EIGHTEEN

Dora

There were two calls she needed to make. Both took some preparation, some thought. But first of all she had to calm down. She'd already scared the shit out of a cabbie and the doorman. *Sixty-eighth and Third* she'd said to the cabbie at the airport and he'd asked her did she want the bridge.

I want you to pick whichever route has the lightest traffic and I want you to find all the holes, she'd said. *I want to get there quickly and efficiently and if you do that you'll get a very good tip out of me and if you don't you'll get the meter. You understand?*

The cabbie had shaken his head. *I love this fuckin' job,* he'd said. *Y'know? I just love the people.*

The doorman had smiled and said welcome home Ms. Welles and asked could he take her bags for her. *The bags are on rollers for a reason, Sergio,* she'd said. *No thanks.* That one she regretted. Sergio had always been fine to her and didn't deserve to be snapped at. She'd apologize to him tomorrow.

But she needed to calm down. Happily there was a half-full bottle of Absolut in the freezer. She poured one and it helped.

The other thing she needed to do was to order her

thinking and get these calls exactly right. Content and tone. The Absolut helped there too. When she thought she was ready she sat down on her bed and dialed.

Barbara answered on the third ring and it was apparent from the voices in the background that she was throwing a little party. Also apparent that she'd had a couple of drinks herself. Turned out that the party was for Barbara's ex. His birthday. Her ex—with whom she'd remained as friendly over the last six years since their divorce as they had been during the marriage. Maybe more so. Toward the end, *definitely* more so. Dora always wondered how folks managed that.

They caught up and talked shop for a few minutes and then Dora hit her with it.

You want me to do what? Barbara said.

"I want you to buy me out. What do you think?"

There was a long pause on the other end and Dora wondered whether it was a good thing or a bad thing that Barb was a little tipsy at the moment.

"Well, I know we'd *talked* about it, I mean, somewhere down the line, but . . ."

"I think now's the time, Barb. I want to try something different for a change. Someplace new. You know, sun, nice weather, that kind of thing."

She could almost feel it slowly sink in.

"Okay, who is he?"

"What?"

She laughed. "This is *Barbara*, honey. Listen, why don't you cab on over and tell me all about him. I've got Liza and Ned of course and Georgie and the rest of the gang over here and we'd love to hear . . ."

"There's nobody, Barb. Honest. I just think it's about time, that's all."

Another pause.

"Okay, okay, there's no guy. If you say so. Come in tomorrow and we'll talk about it. It's kind of sudden. I'll have to think it over. All right?"

"Tomorrow's fine. See you about nine."

"Nine it is. Bye."

"Tell Ned happy birthday for me, okay?"

"Will do, hon. Bye."

She hung up the phone and sat there for awhile and sipped her dirty martini until it was finished and then made herself another and sat awhile longer and then dialed.

And she could hear it in his voice immediately. She pretended she didn't.

Hi, Jim. It's me. I just wanted to let you know I got in all right, and to thank you and . . .

She listened to him.

Oh no. Oh god, Jim. She what? How could she slip . . . ? Oh my god.

She listened some more.

And the kids? What about the kids, are they . . . ?

Jimmy was already on his way home from camp he said. As yet the boy didn't know why. He wasn't about to tell him on the phone. Linda was in her bedroom, clearly distraught. Her best friend Beth was up there with her. He'd go up again himself in a little while.

Listen, I'm going to come right back out there. I've got some business to finish up here tomorrow and then I'll catch the next flight back. This is no time for you guys to be alone. I'll be on a plane by tomorrow, okay? Tomorrow afternoon. I know that. I want to. Listen to me. I want to, Jim. Karen was . . .

And what *was* Karen exactly? She was almost shocked at the very real catch in her throat.

Karen was very good to me. My god I'm so sorry, Jim. Really I am. I'll see you tomorrow night, all right? You take care of yourself in the meantime, will you? And tell Linda and Jimmy . . . just tell them hello for me. Send them my love, all right? Can you get some sleep? Try to get some sleep, okay?

He would. He'd try.

Okay. Goodbye, Jim. Goodbye.

And she was surprised once again by the tear that rolled down her cheek and then truly amazed at the sobs which continued on and off through the night.

NINETEEN
Dora, Matthew, and Linda

There was certainly no shortage of mourners. Karen had a lot of friends obviously if only her widowed mother in the way of immediate family. Dora took in the tableau graveside. Jim rigid and pale in the bright California sunshine holding Jimmy's hand on one side with his arm around Linda's waist on the other. His father Mr. Weybourne had gone mostly bald and had developed quite a paunch since she'd seen him last and he stood behind them, hands resting lightly on Jimmy's shoulders. Mrs. Weybourne, whose hair had gone a beautiful silky white and whom time had treated far better than her husband, attended to the frail old shattered woman who was Karen's mother.

The pastor read from Ecclesiastes. *Or ever the silver cord be loosed, or the golden bowl be broken, or the pitcher be broken at the fountain, or the wheel broken at the cistern, then shall the dust return to the earth as it was: and the spirit shall return to God who gave it. Let us pray.*

She joined the mourners in the Lord's Prayer but did not bow her head as did most. Her eyes stayed on Jim. He was saying the prayer too but his shoulders were shaking. Linda glanced up at him. He turned to her with a small sad smile and the shaking slowly subsided.

Matthew's eyes were on Dora. He'd found himself standing uncomfortably close to her as the group assembled—just behind her and to the right—and by the time he was aware of her there it would have been embarrassing to move away. She looked stunning of course, dressed in elegant black silk.

She was watching Jim with what appeared to be serious concern.

He relaxed slightly. The concern looked real all right. But he still didn't have to like the woman.

. . . and lead us not into temptation, but deliver us from evil. For thine is the power and the kingdom and the glory forever . . .

He followed her gaze and saw Linda press her head against Jim's chest and begin to cry.

She had always found it strange that at the reception after a funeral people ate as heartily as they did. Was it because a funeral was emotionally exhausting, expending energy that the body then needed to replenish? Or maybe it was simply life reaffirming itself. *I eat, therefore I am.* Still *am.*

Whatever the cause the cold cuts were the first to go and as she set a new platter heaped with ham and cheese and roast beef and sliced turkey on the table she saw Linda and Jimmy standing across from her and noted that while Jimmy's plate was full Linda's portion seemed merely a token gesture to hunger.

She smiled at them. Jimmy returned the smile. Linda didn't.

Linda practically glared at her.

Now what the hell was that *all about?*

She watched the girl drift slowly into the living room to join her father and Matthew and some business associates near the front door. The snub was palpable. She felt her cheeks flush and turned to go back into the kitchen with some empty plates, keeping busy her main objective now but Mr. and Mrs. Weybourne seemed to appear out of nowhere in front of her with drinks in hand. His would be scotch, she remembered, hers rye and soda.

"It's so good of you, dear," said the woman. Dora thought the single string of pearls quite tasteful. "I'm really very glad that . . . even under these awful, terrible circumstances . . . we've finally got to see you again."

"It's good to see you too, Mrs. Weybourne."

"We were always hoping, you know, Robert and I . . . I mean, you were so very close once, you and James . . ."

"I know."

She was aware of no other living soul who called him James. Not even his father.

"It's silly, of course, because you were so very young, but we sort of even thought . . ."

"I did too, Mrs. Weybourne. I guess we all did. But we were kids, weren't we."

Her smile was awkward. "Of course. Yes of course you were. And Karen was so good for James, wasn't she. So good."

"Yes. She was. I'm sorry."

And there was nowhere to go after that for either of them.

"Well thank you, dear. Thank you for being here."

Mr. Weybourne nodded his agreement. He was never much for words she thought. As an investment banker she guessed he didn't need to be.

"Least I can do," she said and headed for the kitchen.

What's she doing here? Linda thought. The words kept playing over and over in her mind like some stupid tune you hear in your brain early in the morning that stays with you all day long. *What's she doing here? She's not my mother's friend. She barely knew her. So what the hell's she doing here?*

It might have helped if Beth and Suzie were still around, if she had somebody to talk to—she might have been able to think about something else but Beth and Suzie were uncomfortable in this situation and she couldn't blame them, she'd have been uncomfortable too if it had been one of their mothers who had this stupid fucking accident and died. Her father was busy talking with these men from work and Jimmy was no help. Jimmy was a kid.

So she stood there with this stupid plate in her hand. Cantaloupe and honeydew and sliced pineapple and a fat pair of strawberries.

Fuck food. Fuck this. Fuck everything.

She walked back to the table and practically tossed the plate onto it so that the strawberries bounced off onto the tablecloth. She walked back through the crowd and up the stairs to her room.

What's she doing here?

And Matthew took note of this.
He said nothing to Jim.
Not now.

Dora watched him sip his drink alone and exhausted on the couch. He was not drinking heavily but he was drinking steadily now that the guests were gone. She moved back and forth from the dining room to the kitchen, wrapping meats and cheese and salad, fruits and apple tarts. Finding room for them in the refrigerator. Keeping busy. When she was done she'd start stacking dishes in the dishwasher.

She was good at this. She was very orderly.

"Leave it, Dora," he said. "Lin and I will handle it later."

She rinsed her hands and dried them and went into the living room. Sat next to him on the couch.

"I have a better idea. You go up to bed. Take a nap. How much sleep did you get last night?"

"Not much."

"I want to do this, okay? You take care of your family. That's all you have to do right now."

He looked at her, tears welling up in his eyes.

"My family."

She reached out for his shoulder and then she was holding him, stroking his head, his arms around her tight.

"It's going to be all right."

"She was just . . ."

She heard the unspoken finish. . . . *the most important thing in my life.*

"I know," she said. "We'll take care of it, Jim. You'll see. We'll heal it. You and the kids and me. We'll help. You'll see. But right now you need your sleep. I'll finish up here in a little while and let myself out, okay?"

She pushed him gently away and stood in front of him and reached for his hand.

"Come on. Let's get you up to bed. By the time I'm through you won't even know any of this happened here today."

I'll see to it, she thought. I'll wipe the afternoon clean of everything.

TWENTY

Dora

It took roughly a month and a half for her to become *inevitable*. That was how she thought of it. Not quite death and taxes but close enough.

She proceeded slowly but soon she was preparing the occasional lunch and dinner. She could cook. She'd always been a decent cook. Chicken almandine and Greek roast pork, chateaubriand and quesadillas. Her soft-shell crabs went over nicely with everybody but Linda—she said they looked alive.

But Dora could feel that even Linda was warming toward her.

Once she'd convinced Jim that it was okay to allow her boyfriend Rick over now and then, under supervision of course—Karen had been dead set against that after the petting-on-the-couch episode—the girl had lightened up on her considerably.

Though the entire family was subject to mood swings.

At his Little League games you could never be sure whether, when Jimmy struck out, which he did with some frequency, he'd retire from the plate peacefully or try to smash a hole in it with his bat. Knowing the circumstances his coach complained to Jim as gently as possible. When Linda was denied a one o'clock curfew for some party or whatever it was teens actually did these days she was as apt to go ballistic as not. Even Jim came home from work exhausted but sunny one day while the next all he did was brood all evening.

She guessed it was natural. She simply soldiered through.

One evening the four of them were sitting in front of the television and Jim switched channels to a TMC broadcast of THE GRADUATE, which the kids had never seen. Jimmy never even made it through the pool scene—Dustin Hoffman hiding underwater. That's not funny. I don't see why that's so funny he said and stalked off to his bedroom.

Nobody used the pool anymore. Not even Dora could bear it. A drink outside on the terrace in the sun now and then and that was that. The pool man came to clean it every two weeks.

It was her own imagination she was sure because it was long gone by now but he always seemed to step over or around where the stain had been.

TWENTY-ONE

Linda

Both Beth and Suzie thought it was high time she talked to her brother Jimmy about it and she figured that they were probably right. So that night when she heard the toilet flush she opened the door and stood in the doorway and waited until he padded out into the hall in his pajama bottoms.

"Hey. C'mere," she said.

"Huh?"

"Come on in here."

"What? Into your room?"

"That's right."

He smiled. "You want *me* to come into your room?"

"Jimmy, that's what I said, isn't it?"

He shrugged. She stepped aside and then closed the door behind him.

"Sit."

"Where? Here? On the bed?"

"Of course on the bed, dope."

He looked at her like he was expecting some kind of trick. Like she couldn't be serious. Then sat down on the edge of the bed. She sat down beside him a comfortable few feet away.

"Okay. So what do you think of her?"

"Her? Oh. You mean Dora?"

"Uh-huh. Dora."

He shrugged again. "I like her."

"You do."

"I guess. Why?"

"You don't think she's going all *mom* on us here?"

"That's dopey. She's Dora. She's not mom. Jeez."

"Those high-tops you had on today. Who bought them for you?"

"She did."

"Who bought you the Shadow Ops: Red Mercury?"

"Dora did. She got it on eBay. Said it was cheap. So what? Who bought you the new iPod?"

"I'm not accusing you of anything for chrissake, Jimmy. Yes, Dora bought it for me. You see what I mean? *Dora* did. Not dad."

"Dad almost *never* buys us stuff. You know that. Just Christmas and birthdays. Right?"

"Right. Mom always did. *Now* do you get what I'm saying here, Mr. Thickskull?"

He considered it.

"You mean she's acting like mom did."

"Exactly."

"You really think?"

"I think."

She could see something working on him inside. Finally he shook his head.

"No," he said. "No. That's not true! Mom didn't used to just . . . *give us* stuff!"

He jumped off the bed. Turned to her. Angry and all of a sudden very close to tears.

"Mom used to . . . mom always used to . . . !"

And she truly *felt him* then. A little kid's lonely anguish. Maybe for the first time ever.

She held out her arms.

"Hey, kid . . . c'mere . . ."

"You're wrong! You don't know anything! You're wrong, dammit!"

He flung open the door and ran out into the hall and left her there, heart thudding in her chest by now, hurting for him and for herself too if the truth be known, for the huge empty hole in their lives. She heard his own door slam. Which clearly meant *don't follow.* She wouldn't.

Well, that went well, she thought. *Thanks, girls.*

But it wasn't Beth and Suzie she was really angry with. It was herself. And somehow Dora.

TWENTY-TWO

Jim, Dora, and Matthew

It was a welcome break from the stack of files on his desk but she had never visited him at the office either. So he had to wonder what was up. And when June let her in and closed the door behind her and he looked at her standing there tense and unmoving he knew that something definitely was. His smile didn't manage to elicit any in return. Nor his offer of a cup of coffee. *No thanks.*

"I just came by for a moment," she said. "Could we have some privacy?"

"Sure."

He told June to hold his calls.

"So," he said. "Have a seat, Dora. Relax."

He sat but she didn't. Instead she walked past his desk to the picture window behind him so he had to swivel around to see her. She was frowning, staring out the window. *Practically wringing her hands,* he thought. *What the hell?*

"I've been having some trouble," she said. "I think maybe I ought to go home for a while. Maybe for a long while."

He waited for more but evidently more wasn't forthcoming.

"I don't get it. Why? I guess I mean, why now?"

"Well, there's the business for one thing."

"I thought your partner was handling the business. What's her name?"

"Barbara. Yes, of course she is, but . . . god, Jim. It's not about that. Not really."

"Well what then?"

But he already had a pretty good idea what it was about. He felt a strange mix of sensations. Relief that the cat was finally going to come leaping out of the bag. Dread as to how to handle it once it landed smack at his feet.

"It's us. You and me. Damn it. It's about my wanting you and not feeling right about wanting you. Feeling *horrible* sometimes about wanting you."

She turned to face him.

"We said in my room that night that it had to be the last time. Remember? Because of Karen. But it's not the same anymore, is it. Because . . . my god! I don't know how to say this! Because there *is* no Karen anymore and I don't know what to do with that. I feel guilty and I feel scared and we get closer and closer and it's almost as though I can taste you in the room when you walk by. My god, Jim! Am I awful? Evil? Do you want *me?*"

And he knew what the answer to that one was. There was just no way in hell he could say it to her.

"Do you?" she said softly.

She waited, reached up for the top button of her blouse and then the next and yet a third and he thought *no dear god woman what the hell are you do-*

ing and for the first time in memory he could actually hear the air-conditioning unit because the silence in the room was so fundamental and then could hear the blouse whisper along her arms down to the floor.

She stood before him naked to the waist and watched his face seem to crack suddenly and then he lunged for her, pushing her back onto the windowsill, his cock already hard against her and his mouth on her own. His hands jittered feverishly along her back and then her breasts and as she unzipped him and freed him he clawed her panties down her legs and shoved himself inside her.

You don't go, he said. You stay, you hear me? I'm fucking you. I'm fucking *you!* You don't go *anywhere!*

He pulled out of her and turned her and she pressed her hands splayed against the cool windowsill and raised her ass for him as he lifted her skirt and then he was inside her again and she heard him moan and his thighs slap against her ass and she had the briefest memory of Owen slapping against her too but this was not Owen's bed, this was an office that looked down on the broad sunny boulevard below.

She gazed at the people on the street and the cars across the street in the lot where she'd first seen him again after twenty years and then her eyes focused on her own reflection in the window. She saw Jim's hands clutch her breasts and the sheen of sweat gleam between them and then glanced up at her face and held there. She saw will and a kind of triumph on that face but this was not a person she knew exactly.

A trick of the glass she thought. An abstraction.
One he shouldn't see.

Matthew passed her in the hall standing in front of the
elevator. He gave her a wave and a little smile which
she returned. The smile for once was not dutiful. But it
didn't make him any happier to see it there.

He knew that just-fucked look from long experience.

Jesus jumping christ, Jim, he thought. *What the hell
are you doing? What the hell have you done?*

TWENTY-THREE

Linda

Her father had gone crazy. It was the only explanation she could come up with. He'd gone clear fucking out of his mind. He broke the news to both of them, sitting them down in the living room. And it clearly wasn't open to debate. Fuck that. She debated him anyway.

"For god's sake, daddy! She's only been dead a couple of months! How can you even think this? What the hell are people going to say?"

"Hey. You watch your language, young lady."

"What am *I* going to say?"

"You can say whatever you want, Lin. There's nothing improper here. Nothing to be ashamed of. It's ridiculous for her to continue paying for that hotel room every week. It's costing her a fortune. She's an old friend and we're giving her our spare bedroom, that's all."

"She's an old *lover*, daddy. That's a little bit different, isn't it? An old lover staying in our house?"

"Lin, she's staying. It's a done deal. Okay?"

She looked to Jimmy. Jimmy was going to be no help at all. He just sat there twirling a baseball cap on his index finger.

"I don't see how you can *do* this to me, daddy!"

She took the stairs two at a time and slammed the bedroom door. Damn him! He was going to pay for this. She didn't know how yet but she'd *make* him pay.

TWENTY-FOUR

Dora

She was sleeping later and later and she thought it was because of the dreams. Her dreams had become so vivid she hated to abandon them. She'd had a psychoanalyst once who believed that dreams were reminders of something, big or small, that remained to be accomplished. Of something left unfinished. And she thought that he was right. It was as though she were working on something in her dreams. Only she didn't know just what and she was loath to leave the puzzle for the reality of morning.

And now she'd fallen asleep by the pool in the afternoon sun with her vodka tonic gone warm and flat at her side. In her dream she was in her New York apartment sitting on the couch watching television with a dog she didn't own and a cat she didn't own sleeping on either side of her. The cat was a small tuxedo and the dog a golden.

When the front door opened the golden went on full alert. The cat opened its eyes and blinked and then slept on. A pale blonde woman in a red hooded sweatshirt stepped into the room. Who the hell are you? Dora said and the woman said sorry in a very small voice and turned back toward the door and Dora said it again, who the hell are you? which must have angered the intruder because when she turned again she was no longer a she—she was a large unshaven man with menace in his eyes who took one step toward her and that was when she woke. Grateful this time to leave the dream behind.

She needed a shower.

She climbed the stairs and on the landing heard laughter coming from Linda's room. Male and female. Jim was at work. Jimmy-had a playdate at a friend's house.

Which left exactly who?

She opened the door. *Jesus!* Linda said and pulled her open blouse together but not before Dora had a chance to observe that her nipples were very fair. Rick shrugged his shirt back up over his shoulders

"Get out," she said to him.

"Hey, Miz Welles . . ."

He was trying to apologize.

"I said get out, you little shit!"

And then they were both off the bed and on their feet in front of her, Rick backing away but Linda directly in her face.

"Who the *fuck* do you think you are, Dora?"

"I'll talk to you later, you stupid, *stupid* little girl. I want him out of here!"

"You're not my mother! Who the hell do you think you are?"

"Get out, dammit!"

He moved around her and out of the room as

though she were a downed wire. And maybe at that moment she was.

"Rick? God damn you, Dora! Rick!"

She blocked the door.

"Button your blouse for god sakes. Have some decency. Have some pride."

"How dare you?"

"How dare I? The only reason he's even allowed in the house is because of me. And then you turn around and do this to me? Have you fucked him yet, Linda? Or were you just getting around to that."

"What I do is none of your business. You are *not* my mother, Dora!"

"No. I'm not. Lucky you. You're really very lucky that I'm not."

And she didn't know what the girl was seeing in her eyes but it must have been something because she backed off a little then and began to button her blouse. She felt her own anger subside. Or maybe it got submerged in a sudden sense of her own hypocrisy. Whenever the kids weren't around she was sleeping with their father.

"We are going to try to get along, you and I," she said. "For your father's sake and for Jimmy's. Because I wouldn't want anything to hurt them. Because that's what I'm here for—to make sure that nothing happens to them.

"You really don't understand, do you? You don't realize, Lin, what can happen to you. When you let them. When you give and give and you wait for something back. And it never comes back. I don't want boys or men to hurt you and they will unless you're very strong. I can teach you. You are going to let me teach you. It's nothing you ever wanted to know but it's something you *need* to know. I only want to help you. And you'll let me help you. Won't you."

"I . . ."

"Good."

She felt much better now. She turned toward the door.

"There's no need for any of what happened here to go beyond this room. Your father would be very upset. Very unhappy. Just don't let it happen again. We'll talk, you and I. In the meantime . . ."

She laughed.

". . . if you need to feel hands on your breasts, use your own."

TWENTY-FIVE

Linda

No way she could sleep.

She had never liked Dora but she had never been scared of her either. Now she had the feeling her father had involved them all with a total nutcase. Her words kept repeating over and over. *Lucky you. You're really very lucky that I'm not.* And *I can teach you. You are going to let me teach you.* She had never seen anybody go really postal before. And what was that completely strange business about boys and *when you let them. When you give and give . . .*

Jesus! She needed to talk to her dad.

She was going to get into a world of hurt over letting Rick go as far as she had but she needed to talk to her dad so she got out of bed and padded down the hall to his room and at the threshold the horrible disgusting thought occurred to her that he might not be alone in there. That she might be with him.

But if that was the case she needed to see. And besides, she didn't want to doubt her dad who said there was nothing going on between them so she turned the doorknob as quietly as she could and stepped into the room and in the dim light from the hall she could see that he was alone. He was snoring lightly. She didn't know he snored. Her mom had never mentioned it.

"Dad?" she said.

He didn't wake. And what was she going to say to him, anyway? That she couldn't sleep because she suspected his ex-girlfriend was a fucking lunatic? He'd chalk it up to stress or the shock of her seeing them there like that or some damn thing and she'd still be busted bigtime over Rick. It was a no-win situation.

Maybe Beth and Suzie would know what to do. Bethie was smart as hell. She'd talk to them tomorrow.

At least she'd learned one thing. He wasn't fucking her, thank god.

Not now anyway.

There was a light burning in Dora's bedroom at the end of the hall. She could see it under the door. She hadn't noticed before because she was intent on her dad but it looked like Dora wasn't getting a whole lot of sleep tonight either. Did she have her TV on? She heard a voice or voices.

It was scary as hell because she expected the door to come flying open any second but she tiptoed over anyway. It was only one voice. Only Dora's. Like she was having a conversation but there was nobody there. She could make out some of the words. *I could tell you . . . oh yes . . . what I could say . . . about boys . . . about* daddies . . .

She backed away. Went to her own room and closed the door.

The woman was bent. Seriously bent.

TWENTY-SIX

Matthew

He hated doing this but somebody had to.

Lunch—Jim's Caesar and his Waldorf—remained pretty much untouched but they were doing well with the second scotches.

"What I'm saying, old buddy, is that somebody's not playing exactly straight here. I called every major dealer in L.A. and with one exception they never heard of her. The exception visited her shop a couple years ago in New York. Period. So what's this 'buying trip' stuff all about?"

"Private dealers, maybe."

"Private dealers maybe? Jesus, Jim, you used to wear a *mind* when you went out in the morning. How could she get to the private guys without the majors?"

He had no answer to that one. Just sipped his scotch. Matthew felt bad for him but he still needed to press his point.

"As far as I can see the only people she knows in this town are you and me and your family. Us and some redneck over at Hugo's maybe."

"Redneck?"

"I saw her handing some guy an envelope or something over in their lot one night. They both seemed pretty pissed off at first and then she hands him this envelope. I dunno what in hell it was all about. Hey look, maybe I'm wrong. Maybe he's a 'private dealer,' right? Antlers and antique gun racks. Big market for that kind of thing in New York City."

"This guy. What'd he look like?"

"Like he had a pickup dating from 1967 with human bloodstains in the back. Big guy. Shaved head. Leather. Why?"

"Just wondering."

But he wasn't *just wondering*, Matt could tell. He'd hit some sort of nerve here. Clear as day. But he knew Jim Weybourne and the tone of voice told him he wasn't about to discuss it further. He pushed back in his chair.

"Look," Jim said, "I'm not real hungry. We'd better be getting back."

"Okay, we'll call for the check. You'll think about it though, right? I mean, who is this woman anyway? She's sure not the college kid you remember. I just feel you're making a big mistake here, buddy."

"Don't worry, Matt. I will. I'll think about it."

TWENTY-SEVEN

Jim

He was getting no work done at all. Not a damn thing. He kept poring back over the details of that day in the lot. To hell with it he thought finally and pressed the call button on his desk.

"June? Put me through to a Barbara Tilldon at Welles' Antiques on Madison Avenue in New York City. That's right. T-I-L-L-D-O-N. Thanks."

June was fast and efficient as always. He picked up the phone and asked his questions.

His foot was killing him today and between that and Dora he barely noticed Linda and Jimmy sitting on the couch in front of some cop show until she said hi daddy and knew she saw that something was wrong.

"Where's Dora?" he said.

"Kitchen."

"Do me a favor, will you? Take the show upstairs for a while."

"Ahhh, dad . . ." Jimmy said.

But Linda got it, bless her.

"Come on, dweezle."

She got up and clicked off the television and led Jimmy up the stairs and only glanced back at him once. Still the look was troubled. He walked to the dining room and put his briefcase down on the table and proceeded to the kitchen where she was stirring something that smelled of onions and potatoes and vinegar on the stove.

"Hi," she said. "You're early."

"Turn if off, Dora."

"What?"

"Turn off the stove."

She frowned but did as he asked and put the slotted spoon down on the counter and turned to him.

"I want to know what the hell you're doing here."

"What do you mean, what am I doing here?"

She seemed genuinely flustered and confused.

"I called your partner today. Your ex-partner. She likes you very much and she's very loyal. But she told me about your selling the business right away because she wondered if you were all right. She's concerned because you haven't cashed her check yet and she wondered why. She was also concerned when I asked her what items you'd sent back to her for the shop because she wasn't expecting any. There were business trips and pleasure trips, she said.

"You lied to me. Matthew did some checking. There were no dealers. And no New York buyers."

He waited. She said nothing and it was impossible to read her.

She moved past him into the dining room and sat down at the table. He followed.

"Why?" he said.

She wouldn't even look at him. She only shook her head.

So that was how it was going to be.

"I want to know who the guy was in the parking lot, Dora."

That got her attention.

"What?"

"You set it up, didn't you? It was the night we slept together 'for the first and last time ever,' remember? You had me playing hero out there like a goddamn idiot. How hard was he supposed to hit me, anyway? I personally think he overdid it a little."

"Jim . . . I only . . . I didn't know how to . . ."

And he heard the rest of it clearly in his mind—how to *get to you*—and where he'd come home angry god knows now he wanted to beat the living shit out of this woman for playing him and all of them this way.

"And then jesus, Dora, Karen dies. And suddenly here you are all over me! All over *us* . . . like some leech, like some fucking mother hen! What the hell were you thinking? What is this? *Carpe diem?* And what the hell brought you out here in the first place? After all this time."

She got up and started to move toward him around the table and there was clear misery in her face but he wasn't going wherever she was, misery or no misery, not now.

"Jim, please . . ."

"No! You stay the hell away from me, Dora! Was it me? Did you came out here for *me*, Dora? I think you did."

"No, it was work . . . a working vacation. I tripped over you in a restaurant, remember? It was just an accident."

"Just dumb luck, huh? I don't believe you. I think you're happy Karen's gone. I think you used it. I want you out of here, Dora. I want you out of here *now*."

And she started toward him again anyway the arrogant conniving bitch until he saw her eyes shift to something behind him so he turned and there was Linda standing in the doorway, her eyes cold and hard staring straight into Dora's. He had never seen his daughter like this but those eyes would have stopped a mad dog in his tracks. Dora folded.

"All right," she said. "Okay."

She walked past them into the living room, Linda not even stepping aside for her as she passed so that she lightly brushed his daughter's shoulder. She scooped up her purse off the armchair and headed for the door and then she stopped and turned.

"Your dinner's on the stove," she said. *"I hope you choke on it."*

TWENTY-EIGHT

Laura Foster, Greg Lambert, and Bob and Nellie Bates

She was beating him up the hill again and this time Greg thought okay, let her. On a bike Laura was literally hell on wheels from working out five times a week and while Greg was in pretty damn good shape himself his own sport was baseball and pitchers didn't need the power in their legs that you did in, say, left field. Anyhow he liked to watch her tight little butt shift from left to right and back again as those strong legs pumped away.

So far that butt was all she'd let him touch reaching back inside her shorts unless her breasts outside the shirt counted which he guessed they sort of did but they'd only been together a week now and he knew that would be changing soon. She'd pretty much promised him at Baadeker's party. Let's take our time she said and that was okay with him, he could wait. It was kind of fun to wait and build up to the thing a little at a time. He figured he loved her for sure and that the feeling was mutual. And she was already taking care of those pesky hard-ons.

Laura was a year older than Greg—a junior to his sophomore—and as his parents used to say about Greg's big sister, she'd *filled out nicely*. Which, translated, meant she had a body to die for. She was a transplant from Tennessee and the minute he'd seen her walk into the cafeteria and then heard that incredible silky southern accent coming from the next table he'd fallen like petals off a flower. Then the next day when he reported for his waiter's job at TJ Express there she was putting on her apron.

He figured it was meant to be.

She was distancing him by a couple of yards now though which was way too much even for him so he put on some speed.

Laura decided to give the poor guy a break and eased up a little.

Her mother had taught her that you don't humiliate a man if you expect him to stick around and proved her point over and over again with her father who she certainly could have humiliated easily. Her mother read books and novels in the original French and her father read nothing heavier than the *Wall Street Journal*. Business excepted her mother could think circles around her dad. And she had all the inherent grace and style of a true southern lady while her father was often too hearty, too abrasive, with not a whole hell of a lot of social skills that Laura could see.

They fought like hell sometimes. But never in public.

Her mother wouldn't dream of it. Her mother was a lady.

Laura was no lady. She intended to fuck Greg's eyeballs out when the time was right but that didn't mean the lesson was lost on her. Not at all. So she feigned a bit of fatigue and let him gain a bit. Not too much. Just enough to keep that pride of his intact. You had a man without pride her mother said, you had no man at all.

She knew exactly how to maneuver it so he'd never notice she was faking. You pump with the left foot and list your body a bit to the right, pump with the right and lean to the left. You weren't a bullet anymore. You were slightly off balance and it slowed you up some.

She glanced over her shoulder and saw him gaining to her right near the shrubs and the wide expanse of lawn.

And the car bearing down.

Bob Bates had been making a living writing books and screenplays since the early 1960s but he later thought that never in a life creating fiction had he ever come up with any damn thing like this.

He and Nellie were in front of the house working boxes of pansies into the soft newly turned earth—his wife was always partial to the delicacy of pansies—because at this time of day the dusk would be gentler to them than even sunrise, when he heard a girl scream *look out!* and he turned to see the boy dive off his bike into the Proctors' shrubs one door down and the bike fly off the car's front fender and over its hood and the goddamn car kept coming until it kissed the girl's rear wheel and he shouted *hey! goddammit!* because he could have sworn on his deathbed it was on purpose.

The girl fell hard but he thanked the lord they had an ordinance against sidewalks up here so that it was lawn she hit and not concrete and he heard Nellie gasp and knock over the watering can beside her because the way the girl hit was shoulder-and-head first and then over on her back and to her side and then she stayed that way, her arms over her head like a diver.

Nellie was up before he was arthritis notwithstanding and they saw the hedges shudder and the boy stumble out of them and fall to his knees. They heard the car screech to a halt and a car door slam. The boy was on his feet now his face all bloody from the hedges but the girl didn't move. The boy was lurching toward her but they got there first as she groaned and tried to get up on one elbow and fell back again. At least she's alive he thought and Nellie was saying *honey? honey? are you all right?* bending down to her, her hands all fluttery, the hands not knowing what the hell to do, touch her or not touch her.

The boy went to his knees and said *Laura? Laura?* and then he looked up behind him and they saw his face change so they turned and saw this woman glaring down at them.

What the hell . . . ? he said not knowing why in the world she would possibly look angry and the woman said *Shut up, you! You just shut the fuck up!*

My god you might have killed them! Nellie said and the woman said *I told you to shut the fuck up!* and they did. This was one scary woman here. Something in her eyes he'd never seen before in all his life or dreamt of in all his career and he turned instinctively to the boy who was younger and stronger than they were but the boy was scared too, he could tell. The girl groaned again and tried to get up again and the boy turned his eyes from the woman and helped her and then he had her sitting cradled in his arms. *Laura honey are you all right?* he said, *are you okay?* She nodded a weak little off-kilter nod but Bob saw that her eyes were all jittery. Bob didn't like the look of her. He glanced at Nellie. Nellie didn't like it either. *Call an ambulance, Bob,* she said. *Hurry.*

You're not them, said the woman. Said it real low almost like a growl. He saw sudden tears pool in her eyes and spill over. *You're not even them!* she said and turned and ran back to the car wiping at her eyes. He heard the car door slam shut. And by the time he got to the door of his house she was pulling a crazy U-turn on that half-blind stretch of road in front of the Proctors'.

Speeding away. Going far too fast. Going back the way she came.

TWENTY-NINE

Ensemble

It was happening to her again. It already *had* happened. And it was going to be just the same as this the rest of her life. There was only one way of stopping it and she was thinking hard about that right now.

She pulled into their driveway. Turned off the ignition. Reached into the glove compartment and took out the gun.

Exactly when she'd loaded it she really didn't know.

He heard the car pull in and saw her through the window running toward the door and registered the gun immediately. His goddamn limp was slowing him down and he thought *gun accident gun accident* the past mingling with the present and his fingers found the lock just as she slammed through the door. The door hit his forearm and he felt a bright streak of pain and took one step back before going for her but that was all she needed to raise the gun and fire.

Oh baby, oh Jim she thought but she fired at him anyway trying to aim through the tears, the first shot as her hand rose slamming into his left thigh—his unlucky leg, the leg ending with no toes at all, she'd caressed

that strange misshapen foot when they'd made love—
the second shot going wild somewhere behind him
into the ceiling, the third catching him full in the chest
and putting him down.

She climbed the stairs.

She fired carefully at the lock on Linda's door and
then pulled the door open and there she was.

The 911 operator told her to *stay on the phone, please
stay on the phone* when the window absolutely beck-
oned. And it wasn't that she was such a good girl that
she always bought into whatever some adult told her
to do god knows and it wasn't her fear of falling from
the window so much as she was loath to leave a human voice behind even a total stranger's voice and she
thought of her father and was he still alive or not down
there and was there anything in the room besides the
ceramic bedside lamp she could use against her and
that was when the gun went off again and her lock fell
spinning across the floor so she figured the lamp
would have to do.

Dora hated the girl. Despised her. It was as though a
fog had drifted away between them finally and she
could see clearly now what she'd only glimpsed before, all the promise in her youth and in her future, see
herself at that age still almost new to her period and to
her breasts and her urge to fuck—no, to *make love,* not
to fuck—it was boys who always wanted to fuck and
then of course they fucked you over. She *was* this little
girl who came rushing at her with a blue and white

table lamp raised over her head and it was an easy thing to shoot her and save her all that goddamn trouble forever.

Jimmy cowered.

He cowered in the closet of course. Crouched down there in the dark with the clothes rack overhead, crouched amid his shoes and sneakers and the tennis racket and fishing pole and boxes and boxes of toys and games he was way too old to play with ever again. He was clutching a baseball bat but she knew he wouldn't use it.

Jimmy? she said. *I wanted to be your mommy. Did you know that?*

He wouldn't talk or even look at her but only hunched there amid all these little-boy things that had defined him up till now.

Your daddy wouldn't let me. Linda wouldn't let me. And I think . . . I don't think you'd have let me either, would you. Not in the long run. Not really.

He closed his eyes. Of the three of them Jimmy was the wisest.

She put the gun a few inches from his eye and fired.

THIRTY

Old Flames

"How you doing, Dora?"

"Fine. What are you doing here, Matthew? Jesus."

"I wanted to see how you were taking it."

"Taking what?"

"How you were taking the news. That Jim's dead."

"My lawyer phoned me."

"Of course he did. I know Bob Weber. He's a very good attorney. My educated guess, for what it's worth, is that you'll probably beat Murder One. He's *that* good."

"There's no question I'll beat Murder One. I didn't know what the hell I was doing back there. I damn near took out two kids on their bikes for god's sake."

"Uh-huh. So how *are* you taking it, Dora?"

"I don't know. For him to hold on for over a week. It just seems . . . well, unkind."

"Unkind?"

"It should have been faster. It should have been over."

"Over for who? Jim or you?"

"I don't need this, Matthew."

"I'm just asking. I'm curious. Over for who?"

"For both of us I guess."

129

"Really."

"Yes, really."

"I'm trying to understand you, Dora."

"Why? Why the hell would you want to understand me?"

"Why the hell wouldn't I? For my own reasons. Those people were my friends."

"I know that."

"They let you into their lives. I'd really, really love to know why."

"Linda didn't. Linda never did."

"Okay, so Linda didn't. Jim and Jimmy did, though. And Karen."

"Karen. Yes, Karen."

"Jim loved you."

"You think so?"

"Yes I do."

"You think it wasn't just sex?"

"No. I think he loved you. I think he'd have to love you to do what he did."

"I wouldn't know," she said and looked away from him then. "I've never been in love. My cat. Lawrence. Maybe."

RIGHT TO LIFE

"... endowed by their creator with certain unalienable rights ... among these are life, liberty, and the pursuit of happiness ..."

—*Thomas Jefferson*

"God finds you naked and he leaves you dying. What happens in between is up to you."

—*Robin Hitchcock and the Egyptians*

THE FIRST DAY

ONE

New York City
June 8, 1998
10:20 A.M.

They drove to the clinic in silence.

The night before they'd said it all. Now there was nothing left to say.

It just remained to do it. Get it over with.

Morning rush hour traffic had ended over an hour ago and traffic was fairly light. The streets of the Upper West Side seemed strangely still and dreamlike, the blue-green Toyota van in front of them drifting from stoplight to stoplight like a guide taking them from nowhere to some other nowhere while they followed to no determinate end.

Running on empty, Greg thought. *Both of us*.

The silence turned him back in time to their bed last night in her apartment, making love through a haze of tears which came and went with the gentle anguished regularity of waves at low tide, their very heartbeats muted, the two of them drawn more closely together than they had ever imagined or wished possible in the grim sad knowledge that pleasure now was also pain and would remain so for a very long time. Her tears cooling on his cheek and mingling with his own, the musky smell of tears and then the feel of them falling to his chest as she sailed astride him like a ship on a windless sea and when it was finished, the long dark night embracing in warm attempted sleep.

Then stillness too through the loud morning rituals of water, razor and toothbrush, both he and Sara alone now in these things as they would ever be. Then coffee drunk in silence at the table, Greg reaching out to take her hand a moment across the polished pine to feel the warmth of her again, to bind them for a moment before walking out through the door into the cool bright morning air. To the morning errands of New Yorkers along 91st and West End Avenue, the cars and cabs and delivery trucks. And then down to the car parked deep in the cooler echoing basement garage next door, Greg driving them across to Broadway and then downtown. Bringing them forward along the wheel of time to this awful empty place. This quiet, this exhausted drift of feeling.

"Are you all right?" he said finally.

She nodded.

The clinic wasn't far. 68th and Broadway, only five blocks away. One of only three of them left open on the entire West Side from the Village to the Bronx.

"It's a girl," she said.

And it was that, he thought and not his question that truly broke the silence.

"How can you tell?"

"I just know. I remember the way Daniel felt, even at this stage. This feels . . . different."

He was aware of something thick and heavy inside him again. He'd heard the story many times in the six years he'd known her. Her perceptions of the thing varying slightly over time and distance and depth of understanding. Daniel, her son, dead in a frozen lake in upstate New York at the age of six. Even his body lost to her beneath the ice and never found.

If there was ever a woman he would have wished to have a child with, to have *raised* his child, especially a *girl-child*, it was this one.

His hands were sweating on the wheel.

Because of course it was impossible.

"Why don't you drop me off in front," she said. "Find a place to park. I'll go in and register. Less time waiting."

"Are you sure?"

"The front will be fine."

"What about those people with their goddamn picket lines. They'll probably be out again."

"They don't bother me. Except to piss me off. They'll let me by, don't worry."

He supposed that no, she was not about to be intimidated. Last week going in for her examination there had been seven of them on the sidewalk by the entrance to the Jamaica Savings Bank, the building which housed the clinic and held its tenuous lease, seven men and women standing behind blue police barricades, carrying cardboard signs saying HE'S A CHILD, NOT A CHOICE and ABORTION IS LEGALIZED GENOCIDE and waving pamphlets and holding out tiny plastic twelve-week foetuses cupped in the palms of their hands.

One of them, a surprisingly handsome fortyish man, shoved his own little specimen at Sara's face and Sara turned on Greg's arm and said *you stupid shit* and walked on by past the three policemen lounging at the door who were guarding these creeps on his and her tax dollars thank you very much, and into the building.

Then this other one, this ordinary-looking woman about the same age as the man, who followed them to the elevator and up and sat there with a magazine across from them in the waiting room staring until Sara's name was called and then got up and left. A more subtle form of harassment. Were they even allowed to *do* that? They'd never said a word to her though he'd wanted to. And she'd evidently known what he was thinking. *To hell with her*, she'd whispered, *she's not worth the effort.*

She could deal with them.

Still he'd feel better if he was with her.

"What's another minute or two?" he said. "Let me just park this thing and we'll go in together."

She shook her head. "Please, Greg. I want to get this over with as soon as possible. You know?"

"Okay. Sure. I understand."

But he didn't. Not really. How could he? For all the talk last night it was impossible to gauge how she felt at just this moment. Not now in the light of day, far beyond the familiar comfort of home and bed and the comfort of lying in his arms and even the comfort of tears. He wanted to know suddenly, *needed* to know, that she didn't hate him, didn't blame him fundamentally—though twice last night she'd said she didn't and he'd believed her. But now it was different. He wanted to know she forgave him. For everything. For his marriage. For his son. Even for his sex. For being born a man so that he didn't have to carry—couldn't possibly carry—the full weight of this. He'd have done it in a minute if it were possible.

Her diaphragm had failed them. It happened sometimes. They were adults and they knew that. It was *her* diaphragm. It didn't matter. He'd never felt so guilty in his life.

Do no harm, his mother had told him when he was a boy. The physician's rule. Her personal golden rule. And here he was, doing harm to the woman he loved.

Still more harm.

He could see it in the distance on the corner of 68th Street a block and a half away, an undistinguished grey highrise that was probably built back during the mid-sixties, the bank on the first floor and offices above. Across Broadway a Food Emporium and the huge Sony movie complex. And yes, there were the long blue sawhorses and the two cops standing at the door and people carrying signs walking back and forth along the curb.

"Pull up behind them," she said. "I don't feel like getting out right in the middle of that."

He glided to a stop. She opened the door.

He put his hand on her arm and stopped her and then he didn't know what to say. He just sat there moving his hand slowly over the warm smooth flesh of her arm and then she smiled a little. He saw the worry and sleeplessness that ambushed her just behind the smile. The eyes couldn't lie to him. They never had.

"I'll just be a minute," he said. "I can probably find something on 67th or over on Amsterdam."

"I'll be fine."

She got out and shut the door and he watched her walk away toward the dozen or so people ahead of her moving in circles curbside at the other end of the block and then he pulled out slowly past her and she glanced at him but didn't smile this time, only hitched her purse up on her shoulder. He passed the stern-faced, holier-than-thou types milling across the sidewalk like flies on a carcass and then he turned the corner.

Go on, she thought. You have to do this. You've got no choice.

He's got a wife and he's got a son. You knew that going into this and in your heart you never did believe he was going to leave them. Not until his son was grown. Despite what you wanted to believe and despite what he said he wished to do. Greg was faithful as hell in his own peculiar way. It was part of what she loved about him.

In a way it was a shame just how good they were together. In a way it was almost cruelty. If only it had been just an affair. If there hadn't been love, caring, tenderness, sharing. All of it, the whole ball of wax.

You had it all, she thought. And couldn't *really* have anything.

She realized she'd been thinking about them in the past tense.

Now why was that?

She glanced at him through the window as he drove on by. It was impossible to smile for him again though she knew he needed it. She knew how he was feeling. But a single smile was all she had in her today and she'd spent that currency in the car.

The sound and feel of her heels on the sidewalk seemed to jolt straight through her. The cold hard streets of New York City. She realized she was trembling. A young Hispanic delivery boy on a bicycle shot past her. Going the wrong way, against traffic, and on the sidewalk no less. She shot him a disgusted angry glance that he was moving too fast to see.

Her hands were cold. Her face was flushed. Already she dreaded the picketers moving ahead of her a few yards away. Despite what she'd said to him.

Because this was no examination. This was the real thing.

A life was going to end here.

For a moment she was angry with both of them. *Sara and Greg, playing at love.*

No, she thought. Give the devil his due.

They weren't playing.

And that was the saddest part of all. Because it wasn't fair. Years and years alone after Daniel's death and her shattered marriage and finally someone comes along who's got everything Sam never had and more. Kindness. Consideration. Sobriety. And he loves her. Not just wants her or wants to fuck her but loves her and she loves the man back with a power she finds quite astonishing. And then having to learn all over again that love protected nothing. Love was as necessary to people in the long run as food and shelter but love was also a cruel joke, a trick, both at once, two sides of the same coin. And you never knew when the coin would be turning. Because if it didn't wind up *this* way, wind up stranding you between love and necessity, even if it *did* work out between you, then one of you was going to die before the other and leave you all alone again. Love was also about the death of love.

Like this.

Like killing the child inside, *their* child, who should have been a wonderful child alive and whole and made of all they had together.

Sara even thought she knew when she'd conceived her—on a warm windy beach that night in St. John just three months past, both of them so crazy over each other especially in that place with his other life so far behind him that they were downright ridiculous together, unable to stop touching, stroking, laughing, all through drinks and dinner. And then later making love in the Carribean Sea, the warmth of the waves, the huge gentle womb of stars and sky.

Which led here.

It was as though it were love itself they were killing. *In the eye of her flesh she saw a beautiful baby girl.*

And knowing that the child was there and knowing already the empty pain of the loss of her, so unexpectedly like that other loss so many years ago, here and now on this busy sunny street, she wondered how long she could go on with him afterwards. If this were not the turning point for both of them.

If she weren't killing the child inside in more ways than one.

She'd begun to cry again. A thin haze of tears as she approached the picket lines. She blinked them back instead of wiping them away. These people might notice. She wouldn't give them the satisfaction.

How can you do this? she thought. *How can you be so small and nasty and so monumentally* selfish *as to approach me now, when I've never been so vulnerable?*

But of course they would.

They saw it as their right, their mission.

There were many kinds of evil in the world and as far as she was concerned this was definitely one of them.

She heard a car approach slowly behind her close to the curb, wheels over pebbled glass and gravel. In her peripheral vision she saw the fender and the light blue hood, the driver's-side window and roof and noted that it was a station wagon, one of those fake woodies, maybe ten years old. A city transit bus pulled laboriously around to the left of it. She passed an elegant slim young woman pushing two infant babies in a double stroller. A teenager on a skateboard.

And then the car stopped moving beside her and the passenger door opened in front of her and she felt someone's arm wrap tight around her from behind just beneath her breasts, pinning her arms to her sides while his hand sought and covered her mouth to stifle the protest, the scream, grasping at the jaw so she couldn't bite and then she was shoved inside, his hand still over her mouth and she glanced back to the sidewalk and saw that one of the protesters, a man wearing a dark blue windbreaker, had noticed her, was looking straight at her, was seeing all of this but was saying nothing, not one word to the others nor to the police at the clinic door, astonished by this as she felt a needle pierce the bare flesh of her upper arm and saw that it was the driver, a woman, holding a plastic syringe between her fingers and grimly clutching the wheel with her other fisted hand while the man who'd grabbed her slammed the door.

As darkness descended over all her sudden fears and long familiar sorrow they slowly pulled away.

He walked by an old woman with a shopping cart full of groceries and then past the picketers, barely noticing them this time and past the pair of cops, one male and one female, who were standing at the entrance. He walked through the revolving doors and past the bank's ATM machines to the elevators, got in and punched eleven. The door to the reception room swung open ahead of him and he stepped aside for a young blonde woman in jeans and a tee shirt who smiled at him. Or maybe she was just smiling at the world that day.

At least somebody was happy.

He walked in and the reception room was empty. He thought my god, had they taken her in already?

Was *anything* that had to do with medicine or New York City *ever* that fast?

The receptionist behind the sliding glass windows

smiled at him too. A purely formal smile, meant to be reassuring. *See? We're harmless here*.

"Sara Foster." he said quietly.

She checked her clipboard.

"Yes. She's got a ten forty-five with Doctor Weller."

"He's seeing her already?"

The clock on the wall behind her read ten thirty.

"No, it's a ten forty-five appointment, sir."

"She's not here?"

She shook her head. "Not yet. But if you'd want to take a seat I imagine she'll be along shortly."

"I don't understand. I just dropped her off. Right here in front of the building. Just this minute."

The receptionist frowned, puzzled. "I'm sorry. She hasn't signed in."

Sara wouldn't do this, he thought.

Something's not right here.

"There's a drugstore a few doors down and a smoke-shop just next door to us. Maybe she needed something. Why don't you have a seat and wait a moment. I'm sure she'll be right along."

"Why would she . . . ? Okay. I'll be back."

He took the elevator down.

After the cool of the overly air-conditioned office the summer sun hit him hard and he was sweating as he peered through the open door to the cigarette shop to see nothing but an old man buying a Lotto ticket and then into the drugstore next to that. He looked around him on either side and then scanned Broadway across the street toward the Sony complex and the shoppers in front of the Food Emporium but he didn't see her. He walked around the picketers again and directly to the cops at the door.

"Excuse me," he said. "Did a woman just go inside?"

The female cop was almost as tall as her partner, nearly six feet. Her hair was blonde pulled up under the cap and she stopped chewing her gum the moment he walked up to her.

"Just now? No, sir."

"Did you see a woman, five, maybe ten minutes ago, white short-sleeve blouse, blue skirt, early forties, long dark hair?" He pointed. "She'd have been coming this way toward the building. I dropped her off over there. She has an appointment at the clinic."

The officer glanced at her partner. So did Greg, actually noticing him for the first time. The cop looked shockingly young. He was big and trim but to Greg he looked barely out of his teens. He guessed the woman would have a good ten years on him. The cop shook his head.

"Sorry, sir," the woman said and glanced behind him.

"Is there a problem?" Greg turned and saw a much smaller woman in a brown business suit and baggy trousers. Her tailored white shirt was unbuttoned at the collar so that the tie hung slightly off to one side. She wore no makeup as far as he could tell and the medium-length hair was a frizzy red.

"I'm Lieutenant Primiano, 20th precinct." She produced a wallet and shield. "You said something about a woman?"

"She's disappeared."

"How so?"

"I let her out on that corner. I went to park the car. I

drove past her and around the block and parked on 67th. She had an appointment for ten forty-five and she was headed right here, walking right toward you when I left her but I went inside and the receptionist says she never showed. She suggested maybe the smokeshop or the pharmacy but I just looked in both places and she's not there. This isn't like her. Sara does what she says she'll do. She should be up there."

"You folks have any kind of fight? Quarrel over anything?"

"God, no. We're fine."

He felt himself flush at the use of the word. *They were not fine. Not today.*

But that was their own business.

The woman studied him a moment and then nodded. "Ella, keep an eye on things here a minute, will you? Dean, ask around and see if any of these people noticed her. Your name, sir?"

"Greg Glover."

"This is Officer Kaltsas and Officer Spader. Mr. Glover, let's go on back inside."

She questioned the receptionist and Weller's nurse and then the doctor himself. She was brisk and to the point. It took maybe ten minutes tops but to Greg it seemed forever. Weller volunteered the notion that it happened sometimes, that at the last minute people changed their minds. You really couldn't blame them.

"Not Sara," he said. "She wouldn't do that. Not possible."

When they were outside again she asked the young cop, Kaltsas, about the picketers.

"Nothing," he said. "Nobody saw her. I got a small problem with one of them, though."

"What kind of problem."

"Maybe he's just a weirdo, I dunno. Didn't answer me right away. Something not right, maybe."

"Which one?"

"Bald guy with the beard in the blue windbreaker. With the sign that says PRO CHOICE IS NO CHOICE. Right there."

Greg looked at him. Middle-aged man with thinning hair, parading in a rough circle between two older women.

"Okay. Talk to him again. Get his name, address, phone number. If you can, see that he sticks around a while but go easy. I'm going to take a walk with Mr. Glover, see if we can spot her on the street."

"Will do."

"Have you got a photo of her? Of Sara?"

He dug it out of his wallet. It was his favorite shot, taken on summer vacation a year before on the streets of Jamaica, Vermont, the Jamaica Inn's garlanded white porch in the background. She always hated having her picture taken and was wearing a goofy smile because of that but to him both then and now she looked lovely, her long hair swirling around her face. He had snapped and snapped her that day out of pure, almost adolescent pleasure, until she practically had to scream to make him quit.

She studied the photo and handed it back to him. "She's very pretty," she said. "We'll start with your car. Maybe she went looking for you for some reason. Where'd you park again?"

"Down on 67th."

She began walking slowly downtown. He matched her pace.

"This is crazy," he said. "People don't vanish."

"No, sir. They don't," she said. "I think we'll find her."

Of course they would, he thought. There had to be some normal explanation. Maybe the doctor was right. Maybe Greg didn't know her as well as he thought he did. Maybe she was sitting in a restaurant a block or two away over coffee, wondering if she should go through with this after all, mulling it over on her own.

She never breaks appointments at the last minute and she's never late. She's not secretive and she's never lied to me and she's not a coward.

No. Something's wrong.

You damn well know something's wrong.

He felt the unreality of it all wash over him and for a moment he felt dizzy, almost as though he were about to faint. Twenty minutes ago he was looking for a place to park, an empty meter, pummeled by guilt at what they were about to do. Now he was walking along peering into storefronts, at people coming out of doorways, pedestrians passing, the pour and turmoil of New York. Searching for a glimpse of her. Walking at what seemed to him a crawl when what he wanted to do was run, look everywhere at once. Police in his life all of a sudden while he'd never had previous occasion to say ten words to a cop. And *this* cop, this brisk no-nonsense young woman like a lifeline to him now, his only potential link to Sara. He felt a sudden incredible dependency, as though his life had just spun out of his hands and landed into hers, a stranger's.

His heart was pounding.

People don't just vanish. Not unless they want to.

Or unless somebody helps them.

Whether they wanted to or not.

TWO

She woke in dark and panic.

Her first thought was that they had buried her alive.

That she was in a coffin.

She was lying on her back against rough unfinished wood, thick wood planks to the left of her, to the right of her, so close that she could barely raise her arms to feel that yes, there was more rough wood above, she could smell it. Pine. There was a pillow beneath her head and that was all. Panic raced through her like a breath of fire. She had never been aware of being afraid of tight spaces but she was very afraid of this one.

She balled her hands into fists and pounded. She heard the pounding echo and knew she was in a room then, in some kind of box in some kind of room and not underground at least *not buried underground thank god* because there would be no echo if that were so but the panic didn't recede any. She could *hear* her own fear in the wildness of her heartbeat. She screamed for help. She pounded and kicked at the lid of the thing and side to side at firm unyielding wood and it hurt, they'd removed her shoes and stockings, she was barefoot and it was only then that she realized that her skirt and blouse were gone too, she was wearing only her slip and panties. And that fact too was terrifying.

Why? she thought. What am I doing here?

What do they want with me?

It was cold.

She was not underground but it must have been some kind of basement she was in because it was summer, the day was warm and yet in here it was cold.

Where was she?

She was crying. The tears went cold on her face the moment she shed them. Gooseflesh all over her body.

She kicked harder. Kicked until her feet were sore and maybe bleeding and then kicked and pounded again. Her breath came in gasps through the sobbing.

Calm down, she thought. This isn't doing any good. *Think*. Control yourself, dammit. Concentrate.

Look for weaknesses.

She had maybe two feet between her chest and the lid above. Maybe she could press the lid off. She raised her arms, took a deep breath and pushed with all her might until her neck was straining, the muscles of her arms and shoulders spasming.

It didn't budge.

She let go of the breath and rested. Then took another and tried again.

She brought her knees up under her as best she could until they pressed tight against the lid, trying to get more leverage, took a third deep breath and pushed until finally all her strength leeched out of her. She lay back, exhausted.

The footboard and headboard, she thought. Maybe there. She slid down until the soles of her feet touched wood, the slip riding up her thighs and then drew her arms up over her head, the palms of her hands flat against the headboard. She was sweating now despite the cold, a thin clammy film all over her. She pushed and felt the headboard give a quarter inch and then stop. She relaxed immediately and used her fingers to explore it on either side.

She touched metal. The headboard was hinged to the left. That meant there was probably some kind of lock on the outside. Which also meant the headboard was the entrance. *How had they gotten her in here?*

She lowered her arms and felt around the base of the box opposite her thighs and found a half-inch space between the base and sideboards on either side. On a hunch she pushed off with the soles of her feet and felt the base slide minutely toward the headboard and then stop.

She was on rollers, casters.

They'd *rolled* her in.

Then locked the headboard behind her.

Somebody had gone to a whole lot of trouble planning this, constructing this. *Building this trap for me.*

It didn't change anything knowing that except to scare her further.

Who were these people? Suddenly she was desperate to know.

There was a woman involved. The woman with the

needle. She'd been driving. Why would a woman do this to another woman? How could somebody do that?

She willed herself to stop thinking, to go back to the original plan. The lock might give. It was possible.

It didn't.

She pushed until every muscle in her body was shaking with the strain and that was when the fear set in deep and final so that she lay still, trembling wide-eyed in the dark. Because she had no choice then but to accept the fact that there was no way out until they decided to let her out to whatever purpose they had in mind, which could be to no good purpose because here she was. Half naked. In a hand-built coffin. Alone in the swimming dark.

Or maybe *not alone*.

She heard scratching, light raspings, like claws, something working at the top of the box and growing more and more determined-sounding as she lay there helpless, frozen, listening

Something wanted in.

A *rat?*

She took a deep breath and shouted. *"HEY!"* Why that word she didn't know. The word simply burst out of her, angry and scared, unnaturally loud in that closed space. *Hey!* She listened. Waited.

The sounds had stopped.

The trembling didn't.

What do they want with me? she thought.

Am I going to die here?

Why me?

There was no answer she could think of to any of these questions that wasn't frightening and nothing to do but ask them over and over again while she waited for whatever deliverance would come in whatever form, in however vast and slow an eternity.

The scratching sounds did not return. The cold did not relent.

Greg, she thought. *Somebody. Find me.*

I'm here.

THREE

Was it day or night?

She was so cold. Colder every minute. She was thirsty. Her throat was sore from screaming, her hands and knuckles raw from pounding.

What time was it? How long had she been here?

Inside the box there was no benchmark for time, nothing to do but wait and think, thoughts turning in on themselves like the track on a model railroad, like the double-ring symbol for eternity, the snake swallowing its tail.

Why me? bled seamlessly into *what do they want from me?* which dovetailed into *is anyone looking for me, searching* or *when will I get some water or see some light* or a thousand other questions which all came down to one question, *how will I get out of here? Alive. Sane.*

She felt permanently stunned to find herself here. The feeling colored all reality. As though suddenly she were not even who and what she thought herself to be anymore. The Sara Foster she knew had come unstuck, uprooted from everything that grounded her. The Sara Foster who taught English and drama to LD kids at the Winthrop School on 74th Street, who was daughter to Charles and Evelyn Schap of Harrison, New York, lover to Greg Glover and pregnant with his child, who was once the mother of a wonderful beautiful boy drowned in a lake, who was ex-wife to Samuel Bell Foster and best friends with Annie Graham since childhood—all these people who had cradled her identity in embraces loving and not so loving for as long as she could remember meant nothing here. Were now almost irrelevant. What mattered was not the known world but the unknown world beyond the box.

These people.

They mattered.

What the dark held mattered. The meaning of the box.

And when she heard the footsteps on the wooden stairs they mattered. So that her heart began to race and the air seemed to thicken so she couldn't seem to get her breath, worse as she heard them on the landing and then move toward her, shoeleather scraping concrete and she began to twist and turn inside the box in a frenzy to get out of there to whatever freedom or whatever fate those footsteps might imply, clawing at the box, slapping at the box, her voice a shrill high-pitched squeal in her ears and while still she gulped for breath. And when she heard the man's laughter at the sounds of her fear and struggle and heard his fingers rattle the lock outside the headboard, rattling it again and again, playing with her, her body betrayed her utterly and she saw a sudden burst of red and fainted away.

* * *

He lifted her out and placed her on the bare stained mattress. Studied her a moment.

She didn't move. She wasn't faking.

He lifted her head and set it carefully into the headbox.

Then he clamped it shut.

The headbox was half-inch plywood about the size of a hatbox, split in two and hinged at the top, with semicircular neck-holes carved into its base on either side and a padlock to secure the halves together. It was insulated and carpeted inside. It muffled all sound, shut out nearly all light.

He'd tried it on himself.

It was scary.

The red plush carpeting pressed close to your face, sending your breath right back at you no matter how shallow your breathing. It was hot and claustrophobic. About ten pounds of weight sitting on your shoulders. And once it was on there was no way in hell you could get it off again. It was sturdy. You could bang it against a concrete wall all day long and do nothing but buy yourself a concussion.

He'd done a good job on this one.

The first two tries were failures. The problem was mostly weight, too much or too little. He'd built the first out of quarter-inch ply and when Kath tried it on she pointed out to him that if you pressed your face into the carpeting and held it that way, making space between your head and the back of the box so you didn't bash your brains in, one good slam against a wall could crack the plywood.

She proved this by demonstrating.

Back to the drawing board.

He built the second box of three-quarter-inch ply and it was tough as nails. But the damn thing also weighed about twenty pounds. You fell with that on, it could snap your neck.

The new box halved the weight. Ten pounds was still a lot and he'd have to watch for that but he felt satisfied it was manageable.

Kath had worn it all day long once just to see. She hadn't wanted to but he explained to her that a trial run was a necessity. He knew she hated the thing from the minute he put it on her. Knew it scared her, made her dizzy and sick to her stomach and later she said it pinched her neck all the time she was in there but that was just too damn bad in the long view, somebody had to try it and it wasn't going to be him. Besides the point was could a woman wear it all day long, not a man. Could a *woman* stand it.

When he let her out at dinnertime her collarbone and shoulders were chafed red and sore and she complained about a stiff neck for nearly a week. Nothing that wasn't going to go away. The point was that yes, it was manageable.

He smiled. If Miss Sara Foster here thought the Long Box was scary—and she obviously did—wait till she woke up again and found herself in *this* one. He'd have put her in the thing in the first place but he was afraid she might vomit from the pentothol. And vomit was easier to clean off the base panel of a pinewood box than to get out of carpeting.

He'd have to keep an eye on that too. On the vomiting. Kath had said the headbox was stifling and made her queasy in and of itself, never mind the Pentothal.

He slipped her wrists through the black leather manacles and pulled each of the straps tight and threaded the ropes through the silver rings attached. The ropes depended from the a pair of pulleys at the top of each arm of the brand-new X-frame he'd constructed for her. Taking the two ropes together he slowly and carefully hauled her up until only her feet rested on the floor, legs slightly bent beneath her. Her head lolled forward heavily so that the box now rested on her breastbone. That probably hurt but as yet, not enough to wake her. He tied the ropes off quickly to the the climbers' pitons hammered into the concrete floor and then stepped forward and slipped a small brass hook screwed into the headrest he'd attached to the X-frame through the corresponding eye at the back of the box so that her head would stay upright and take the weight off the back of her neck.

He'd thought of everything.

He stood back and looked at her. All his creation.

You couldn't see her face and that was good. Control was important. And she was very pretty.

He needed to control himself now.

The only thing that remained at this initial stage was to finish undressing her but he'd wait until she woke for that and was able to feel the cold blade of the knife cutting away her slip and panties. That kind of control was very important too.

Afterwards he and Kath could come down and have some dinner and watch her, see how she took it all and he could go over again with Kath what the next step was supposed to be so there'd be no fuck-ups, no misunderstandings. This he'd do daily. There was a progression of events to this that he needed to be sure Kath would follow. They could speak as freely down here in front of her as they could upstairs. Sound not only didn't get out of the box it didn't get in much either.

He watched her stir. A wrist move slightly, a squeaking sound inside the new leather manacle. The box shifted an inch to the right about as far as it could shift.

She was waking.

FOUR

And now there was nothing in her life but terror.

Her legs and arms were manacled and she knew what that meant. She'd read enough in papers and magazines. Seen enough on the evening news. She was in the hands of some sex freak and dear god, she was probably not the first. Not the way he'd worked this out. There was somebody out there beyond her own vivid dark who liked to hear screams and pleas and whimpers. Before they killed.

Invariably they killed.

She knew that too.

She was aware of the terrible frail vulnerability of her body, of her cold nearly naked breasts, her exposed bare arms and legs against the scratchy wooden beams. Inside the box her eyes could not accommodate the dark. The heavy air was suffocating. She could smell her own breath. Sweat stung her eyes. She blinked to clear them and finally closed them while her body heaved with sobs that were wholly beyond her control wrenched from deep inside her. She heard her own quick gasps for breath. They never seemed to satisfy her aching lungs or still her pounding heart.

She felt the heavy weight at her collarbones.

The chafe of leather on wrists and ankles.

Then the cold touch of metal just below her right wrist, sudden, seemingly out of nowhere. Felt it travel from wrist to elbow-joint and stop there. Then from elbow-joint to armpit, slowly, a sharp prick at the delicate flesh there of a knife or sharp scissors and then travelling again, exploring the slope of breast to pause and prick once more at her fear-swollen nipple, her body jerking back then and the blade moving down again sliding over her trembling stomach to her navel and stopping to poke her harder this time at the tender fleshy remains of what once had linked her to life and then moving on.

She felt rough fingers graze her shoulder pulling away the strap of her slip and then felt that side go slack against her breast and fingers on the other shoulder and then the slip falling softly away across her thighs. The blade inserted itself thin and cold between her panties and the flesh of her hip on the right and she felt it pull and cut and now she was completely exposed to the room and the knife and the man who was doing the cutting, the fingers were a man's fingers she thought, felt herself choking inside the box on tears and mucus, then felt the left side go.

She was naked but for the box. But for the insanity of the box.

Naked and against all reason ashamed to be.

She was glad he couldn't see her face reflect her shame.

And feeling that shame despite the fact that her body had done nothing to cause it, that she had done nothing to cause it, feeling that made her angry. So that the first harsh access of fear began to bleed and blend and fade into stubborn black anger and finally to a strange defiant pride which was the other side of shame.

She hung suspended. Open.

Waiting.

"Lady's got guts," he said.

Kath agreed. Though she said nothing, merely watched him take a bite of the half-eaten tuna sandwich, chew and swallow. And then munch at the potato chips which surrounded it on his plate.

The cat sat in front of them near the X-frame, glancing back at the woman naked on the frame and then nervously at each of them, interested in their sandwiches, wondering who to try to hit up for a bite of tuna, but also clearly interested in this strange new arrival standing here. Stephen was eating while Kath as yet was not. She figured the cat would eventually make her move on Stephen.

It was just The Cat. It had no name. Last summer there'd been moles in the back yard ruining the lawn and they'd noticed the occasional water rat down by the brook. So they'd got the cat from the ASPCA to drive the moles and rats away and the cat was successful at that in an amazingly short time so they decided to let her stay, figuring that if moles tried once they might just try again. The cat was the color of champagne with streaks and spots of white, with one almost-perfect circle of white behind each of her front haunches. Neither of them really cared much for cats but they fed her and paid for her shots and put up with the dead or dying birds or mice she brought home now and then, dropping them on the back porch like some disgusting present.

She watched the cat inch toward Stephen. She'd been right about the cat's decision. Stephen looked up and saw her and kicked at the air in front of her and she was only a cat but she wasn't stupid. She backed away. Sat back and seemed to ponder her luck with Kath.

She took a bite of her sandwich and thought that it definitely needed more mayo. She was actually surprised Stephen hadn't started complaining. But they were out of mayo. She'd forgotten to put it down on the shopping list again.

She was forgetting too much lately. He was always telling her and she thought he was probably right.

Maybe it was stress or something. She didn't know.

But she agreed with him that this Sara Foster person had nerve. Was probably not going to be all that easy to subdue and subvert. She knew first-hand what the headbox was like and to have calmed down so fast took guts all right.

She wondered if he'd chosen correctly.

Though for some reason he was sure he had. *Intuition*, he said. *The way she walks.*

Follow her. Get her name.

"Did you phone in all the stuff to Sandy like I said?"

She nodded.

"What'd he say?"

"He said no problem, give him an hour. The mom

and dad's phone number are probably a New York exchange, he thought maybe somewhere in Westchester or Long Island. The Winthrop School is definitely Manhattan. So he'll get us the street addresses on those and trace her boyfriend's plates. He asked was there anything else and I said I guess we'd get back to him."

"Good. We'll go through the rest of her address book tonight, see if there's anything else we can use."

"Jeez, Stephen. I wanted to watch that *movie* tonight."

She took another bite of the sandwich. Wished it had some chopped celery in it. The damn thing was way too dry.

He glared at her.

"Couldn't we go through her book *after* the movie?"

"No, we couldn't go through it *after* the movie. Can't you fucking prioritize?"

She wished he wouldn't use that voice with her. That condescending tone.

She knew better than to argue with him *per se*. But she wasn't exactly ready to let it go at that either.

"You were going to get the VCR fixed. I mean, I could've taped it."

"*Fuck* the VCR! Jesus! What's more important, Kath? This or your goddamn movie? Do you realize what we've done here? Do you remember what's going on? Do you realize how *important* this is?"

Important to who? she thought. But she didn't want to say that to him either. It was an ego thing and she didn't want to insult him. Stephen prided himself on being a careful hunter and a good profiler of people and a very organized personality. He thought that he had managed this pretty much perfectly so far. He also thought that it *was* important, that it wasn't just a matter of his own satisfaction.

She wasn't so sure about that part.

He saw the look on her face though and relented.

Good. She really *did* want to see the movie.

"What's it called?" he said.

"It's an HBO Original Movie. It's called COVEN and it's based on a book I really liked a lot."

The cat made up its mind and walked over. She picked off a pinch of tuna and held it out to her. She didn't much like it anyway.

He sighed. "All right," he said. "*After* the goddamn movie. But you've got to get more serious about this, Kath."

"Jeez, Stephen. How much more serious can I get? I drove the car, I brought home the Pentothal from the hospital, risked my job, risked *arrest*. I shot her up for you for godsakes! I'm in this up to my neck, y'know what I mean?"

The cat was looking for more tuna. She picked off a chunk and dropped it on the floor. The cat purred and set in.

"I know. But from here on in everything's got to go by the book. *Exactly* by the book. And it's going to be a very long haul. We've got to be diligent as hell."

"Don't worry. I will be."

She got up and walked over to his chair and bent over and kissed him. He smelled like tuna and Old Spice aftershave. She glanced at Sara Foster five feet away, still breathing hard but managing to control it, a bead of sweat rolling down off her collarbone from inside the box. She thought that for a woman her age Sara had a damn good body. Her pubic hair was bikini-waxed, unlike her own. She thought she'd like to get that done someday but there was never enough money around for extravagances like a bikini wax. The tan-line from her two-piece was very clear. Forget about the clumsy headbox and she was very attractive. Made her feel sort of dumpy, to tell the truth.

All this and fertile, too, she thought.

She wondered if Stephen was going to keep his promise about not having sex with her. Not real sex, anyway. If he'd be able to do that.

He'd better.

"How long you going to leave it on?"

"Well, I've got to get her out of the cuffs in about an hour or she's going to have problems with circulation. But by then she'll be hurting and compliant enough so that she won't be hard to handle. I figure we'll just tie her to the chair here and you can hold her head still for me while I take off the box and blindfold her from behind. I don't want her to see us yet. I want us to stay anonymous. We'll turn off the lights and leave her an hour or so and then I want to come back and try to feed her. I'm betting she refuses. So then we put her up on the rack again and I'll give her her first beating. Show her what things are going to be like from now on. She'll get the idea."

"What if she doesn't? Refuse I mean."

He grinned. "If you were in her shoes, would *you*

accept food from us right now? But even if she does, fine. Establishes dependency. Either way we can't lose."

She collected his empty plate off his lap. The cat tried to nuzzle her leg but she stepped away.

Dumb animal.

"Are you going to stay down here a while?"

He nodded. "I want to make sure she's basically okay, that she doesn't throw up inside the box or anything. I'll hang around. But you go on ahead. I'll give you a yell when I need you. If Sandy calls let me know."

"Okay."

She walked upstairs through the doorway that led to the dining room and kitchen and put the plates in the sink and rinsed them and stacked them in the dishwasher. Outside the window over the sink a pair of jays were harassing a small flock of sparrows attempting to feed by the cherry tree next to the garage, diving at them from the white birch on the opposite side of the lawn. Scattering them but making no real effort to feed. Just flying back to the birch and perching there until the sparrows returned and then diving back down to scatter them again. Seemingly just for the hell of it. Or maybe it was the sparrows themselves the jays were after.

Were bluejays predatory? She didn't know.

Nowadays, who wasn't?

In the basement he thought of all the things he would do to her before she broke, all those things which would make her break in the course of time. It would take time he knew and that was fine because the good part was in the breaking. Once the will to resist had disappeared they were like herd animals, like cattle, without motivation other than to go on living with a minimum of pain. The pleasure was in the taming of the will and the mastery of the spirit and he was only in the second true hour of that, the second true hour of all that lay ahead yet already his hard-on was irresistible so he grasped it in his warm calloused hand and looked at her breathing flesh just a few feet away and stroked and stroked.

The cat sat watching him. The cat made him uncomfortable.

He wished it would go away.

When he was finished he went to the sink to wash the scum off his hand and remove the smell of his body and sat down and gazed at her again.

Screw HBO. He had his own Original Movie. Right in front of him.

It was going to go on and on.

FIVE

"I don't want it," she said. "How many times do I have to *tell* you? Please. Just let me out of here. Why can't you just leave the blindfold, let me get dressed and drive me back where you found me? Or *anywhere*. My god, I'm not going to tell anybody. How can I? I don't even know who you are or where I am!"

"Eat your sandwich," he said.

"Please. I *can't*. Just the smell of it's making me sick!"

"When I tell you to do something you do it. I don't care what it is. You understand?"

"You want me to throw up? Is that what you want?"

"I don't care what you do as long as you do what I say and eat the sandwich. Now take a bite."

He held it under her nose.

Tuna salad.

She wasn't lying about vomiting. She felt like a drunk at the end of a long night on sweet cheap wine. Waves of nausea rolled through her, making her sweat. It was worse than being inside the box. She shook her head side to side, trying to escape the reek of it. It was all she *could* do. The leather manacles were attached

172

tight to the arms and legs of the chair. There was a rope around her shoulders and another around her waist.

"Please!"

She began to cry again beneath the blindfold. The blindfold her only garment now. How long and how often could you cry before it was impossible to cry anymore? Did tears have a physical limit? She hoped they did. Like her nudity the tears shamed her.

He shoved the sandwich roughly to her closed lips. It crumbled. Cold clammy bits of bread and tuna falling across her chest and thighs. Some of it clung to her lips. She sputtered it away.

He sighed. She heard a plate set down on a table. He walked around behind her.

She felt the rope around her waist fall free and then the one around her shoulders. He drew them off her.

"Maybe you're right," he said. "I guess this isn't working. I thought maybe you'd sort of get into all this. Some people do, you know." He sighed again. "I guess we'll just take you back like you say. You sure you won't tell? I mean, you promise?"

Some people get into this? Was he crazy?

"I won't. I swear."

"You remember what we look like?"

"No. I mean, it was so fast. How could I?"

He seemed to think about it.

"Good. Okay. I guess we'll do it then. Too bad though."

One by one the manacles fell free from the chair legs. She felt a sudden surge of hope. Maybe if he *was* crazy, he was also crazy enough to take her out of here. Let her go. Give her up. Or even if he had something else in mind, something she didn't even like to think about, there still might be a chance to get free. Everything, every hope, began with getting out of here. Beyond that she'd take her chances. It occurred to her that he could kill her just as easily here as anywhere. Easier in fact.

She was healthy and strong. Anything but this she might possibly deal with.

She felt something brush her ankle. Suddenly wet then smooth and soft. She jumped.

"What's that?"

"The damn cat. Don't worry. Hey! Outa here!"

He released the manacles from the chair arms. She moved her wrists and jangled the rings.

"Aren't you going to take these off?"

"In a minute. First I have to go upstairs and get you some clothes. I sort of ruined the ones you were wearing, you know?" He laughed. "Got to make sure you don't try to run away on me in the meantime. Stand up."

He took her hand. His was hard and calloused. Not a big hand but definitely a laborer's hand.

"Come with me. Over here. Nice and slow. Be careful."

He led her blind across the room. Then he stopped her and raised her hand and snapped it to a ring on the X-frame. Suddenly she was scared again.

"No, wait. You said . . ."

"Just for a minute. While I get you some clothes."

He raised her other hand and attached that too so that she was facing the frame, arms spread wide above her. She heard him step away. At least her legs were free, she thought. Not like last time. For a moment there was only silence.

She heard a whistling sound and fire climbed her shoulder.

She jumped and screamed. The pain settled slowly into a stinging glow, a thousand tiny pinpricks along a fireline of hurt.

"*Fooled you,*" he said.

Then suddenly the blows were coming furiously, fast and hard across her back and buttocks and arms, the tender flesh of her underarms, across the backs of her legs and thighs, then even her breasts and stomach as she tried to twist away, the whip finding the same burning places over and over, uncanny, lighting them with bright new pain like lines of bee stings, like lines of biting ants, no matter how hard she tried to evade him, her wrists burning too scraped raw as she twisted inside the manacles, and whatever he was using it was bloodying her, she could feel the wetness *inside* the pain that was nothing whatever like the feel of sweat though she was sweating too, every muscle straining, bruising herself as she jerked and twisted against the heavy boards of the X-frame. She could hear him grunt with the exertion and her own gasps for breath, the blows *crackcrackcrackcrack* like pistol shots in her ears and it was like there were two of him, three of him, four of him, coming at her from everywhere at once.

Ah ah ah ah! she heard and it was her own voice leaping startled out of her at the fall of each blow, mixed with a high whining keen and that belonged to her too though she'd never heard her voice or any voice make a sound like that. She could take no more *no more* and she twisted from yet another blow to her anguished shoulders and the whip found her breast again burning across it like a laser cutting deep and *PLEEEEEESE!* she screamed, not in protest nor even begging but a prayer to the grim gods of pain, the gods of the body's disaster.

He stopped. She heard him breathing behind her.

"You'll get that every time you disobey. Each and every time. And worse," he said.

From her calves on up her body trembled from the sheer effort of standing. Somehow she found a voice.

"Why? Why are you doing this to me? What did I do to you? I didn't *do* anything."

"Oh. You're innocent? Is that it?"

"I . . ."

"Let me tell you something, Sara."

She started at hearing her name. Almost as though he'd hit her again.

"That's right, I know who you are. And I didn't just lift your name off your driver's license either. I know plenty about you. But we'll get to all of that later. Let me tell you something. The only innocent on God's green earth is an *infant*, Sara. A baby. Some people would say an *unborn* baby. But I'd extend that to, say, the first six months of life or so. In my own opinion. What's your feeling on the subject?"

"I . . . I don't know. I . . ."

"Let me ask you something. What were you going to

do with *your* unborn child? Your baby. Your *innocent?*"
He laughed. "I know perfectly well what you were going to do with him. You were going to let some fucking
Jew doctor kill him and flush him down the toilet. Now
that's real nice. I don't think that makes you exactly an
innocent yourself, do you? I honestly don't think so.
Plus you had to do a little fancy fucking in order to get
yourself knocked up in the first place, didn't you? And
I don't see any wedding ring on your finger. So you tell
me. Who's innocent here?"

She heard a series of snapping sounds and realized
that he was taking her photo. Walking around her, getting her from various angles. She heard what sounded
like him opening and closing a drawer behind her and
then heard his footsteps approaching.

"This won't hurt," he said.

And then his hand was moving over her, rubbing
some viscous scentless lotion over her shoulders, down
across her back and waist. The relief was immediate.
But he was wrong about the hurting. In a way it hurt
like hell. When he got to her buttocks it hurt and when
he got to her breasts. It hurt that this sick son of a bitch
should be touching her in these places and that she
had no say in the matter. She was learning that there
were realms of hurt she'd never imagined.

"You're doing this because I . . . ?"

"I'm doing this *because I can*, Sara. Get that through
your head. Because I can. But yes, I also have an agenda.
Let me tell you how it's going to be," he said almost
gently. "Have you ever heard of the Organization?"

"No."

"I didn't think so. Open your legs."

She'd been holding them tight together. She didn't want him touching her there. The whip hadn't touched her there thank god so there was no reason and even if there were a reason she . . .

"I said open them. Do you remember what happened to you just now? Just a couple minutes ago? You want me to turn you around maybe, try the other side?"

She uncrossed her legs and braced herself, shivering. She felt his fingers smooth the salve over each of her upper inner thighs. His fingers coarse, the salve soothing. But the fingers went no further. They left her alone there.

"That's good," he said. "You're cooperating. I could have forced you. But that's not what this is about. This is about you doing what I ask you to do because I ask you."

She felt him stand and heard him walk around in front of her.

"I'm not going to tell you much about the Organization right now. Except to say that the Organization has a very long reach. And that you're involved with it now, like it or not. Just like I am. I told you I know a lot about you. Well, here's just a little part of what I know.

"Your full name is Sara Evelyn Foster. You were born Sara Evelyn Schap in Boston, Massachusetts, on September 6th, 1955. Your parents are Charles and Evelyn Shap of 221 South Elm Street in Harrison, New York. Your mother is sixty-eight and your father's seventy-two. You teach learning disabled kids at the Winthrop

School at 115 West 77th Street in Manhattan. You've got a boyfriend named Gregory Glover who lives at 224 Amity Street in Rye and who dropped you off for a ten-forty-five appointment this morning with a Dr. Alfred Weller, to abort your three-month-old fetus. How am I doing?"

Her head was swimming. *How long had he been stalking her?* To know this much?

"How can you know all that?"

"It's not what I know personally, Sara. It's what the Organization knows. And believe me, we know plenty. This is nothing but the tip of a very big iceberg. But the point is what I said before. That we've got *reach*. And we get what we want, one way or another. So don't think you're in this alone. You're not. Your mother and father are in it. Glover's in it. Your kids at the Winthrop School are in it. Along with plenty of others. This is not just *your* problem.

"So it all depends on you, Sara. If you do exactly as I say you'll not only avoid another beating like this you'll be keeping a lot of other people you care about safe and sound and out of some very deep shit."

"Why? *What is this about?*" She was practically screaming at him. She couldn't help it. It was crazy! She felt like a receiver on overload, could practically smell her fuses burning. "*What do you want* from me?"

"I want you to calm down, for starters." He sighed. "Look, I've got some stuff that needs taking care of. I'm going to take you down, put you in the Long Box again. You can rest."

How could she rest?

"You're not going to give me any trouble, are you? If I take you down? Remember what I said. The lives and safety of a lot of people are depending on exactly how you handle this."

Could all this *possibly* be true? Could there really be some kind of Organization out there waiting to pounce on her parents or Greg or the kids? Or was this some invention of his, something he'd made up just to scare her?

All this planning, she thought. So much planned ahead of time. The coffin—what he called the Long Box. The whipping frame. That horrible confining *thing* he put over her head. The abduction itself, so fast and clean. They'd targeted her specifically. Could there be something to what he was saying?

Then the woman. Who was she? Part of this Organization, whatever it was? The woman hadn't made an appearance since the car to her knowledge.

She remembered the quick deft plunge of the needle.

She needed more information. A lot more. Right now it wouldn't do any good at all to resist him.

"I won't give you any trouble."

"Good. Do you need to go to the bathroom? I can bring you down a pan."

"No."

When he'd uncuffed her and was leading her across the room she asked for some clothes but he refused. He told her she could take off the blindfold once she was inside and that he would tell her when it was okay to do that but that she'd have to keep it handy and put it on before he let her out again. She asked him for a blanket because it was cold in there and he handed her one made of light cotton, thin and soft like a baby's blanket and she wrapped it around her against her nudity as she lay down on the sliding board and he began to push her in. And then she had to ask him one more time.

"Please. What do you want from me? What do I have to do?" she said softly.

"Lots of things," he said, no harshness in his voice either. Almost as though he were somehow in league with her now.

"You'll see. Most of it won't all be as bad as today. Though I have to be honest with you, some of it will probably be worse. I know how these things go. But it's all for your own good, believe me. I'm not so bad. You'll find that out in time. After a while everything will be fine. I don't want to hurt you any more than I have to, Sara. Honestly."

He slid her into the dark.

"Why would I?" he said. "You're pregnant. You're going to be a mother. *You're going to have a baby.*"

He went upstairs and saw Kath on the couch with a bag of potato chips open in her lap.

"How's your movie?" he said.

"Good. Book's better, though. I don't like some of the casting."

"I decided to go through her address book myself. I want to get back to Sandy soon as possible."

"Did she buy it?"

"It got her thinking, that's for sure."

He went into the bedroom and opened the closet door and took Sara's purse off the floor in back and fished around inside for her book. He sat down on the bed. He took a notepad and pen off the night-stand, opened the book and began making notes. Half an hour later he had what he wanted. He dialed Sandy.

"What's up, old buddy?"

"I've got some more stuff I want you to see if you can find out for me. Got a pen?"

"Hang on a sec. Okay. Hit me."

"First, her parents. Can you find out what her father does for a living or if he's retired or what? Any way to do that? Also if the mother works or did work?"

"Sure. IRS records."

"You can do that?"

He laughed. "You hurt me, old buddy. Easy as getting the clinic's files."

Sandy was probably one of the top two or three hackers in the State of New Jersey, had been ever since high school when he'd break into the school computer on a regular basis and rearrange grades for his friends. It was a game to him back then. Still was. But Stephen practically owed him his diploma.

God knows what he's hacking into now, he thought. The FBI? He decided he didn't want to know.

In that way they were a lot alike. Sandy never even watched the TV news. For a guy with the ability to do damn near anything computer-wise, to peer into any electronic corner, he had very little curiosity. Which made him fine for Stephen's purposes.

"Okay, then this Glover guy. What's he do for a living."

"Already found that. He and his wife run a travel agency in Rye. The company's online."

"His wife? He's married?"

"Her name's Diane."

"They have kids?"

"I don't know but I can find out for you. What's this all about, anyway? Why are you so interested in these fucking people? Playing amateur detective?"

"You really sure you want to ask me that, Sandy?"

He laughed again. "Nah. What're friends for, right?"

"It's nothing illegal. I can tell you that much."

"Did I ask if it was illegal? So. Anything else?"

And that was the extent of Sandy's curiosity.

"Yes. Two names. Annie Graham at 914-332-8765. And I guess this is a sister or maybe an aunt—Linda Schap. 603-434-9943."

They were the only two names listed in the book without an accompanying address so he guessed she must know them by heart. That meant these two were probably close to her. He needed people who were close.

"That last one's a New Hampshire exchange," Sandy said.

"Okay, but I need the addresses and anything else you can find out for me. I also need her teaching schedule at Winthrop. And a list of her students if possible."

"Easy. School computer. Hey, just like old times, buddy boy!"

"Just like old times."

He hung up and joined Kath on the couch for the tail-end of the movie. Gory shit.

Not bad.

She'd finished the goddamn chips though.

THE SECOND DAY

SIX

She dozed and woke, dozed and woke again over and over as though she were in the grip of a high fever, her mind shut down to expectations, possibilities, danger, even to the reality of where she lay. It was as though she were waiting for something, some sign that life could once again return to normal. Until then she would remain dreamless, thoughtless, suspended in the moment. It was not something her will imposed. Her body imposed it for her.

On the last of these wakings she heard a sound, dim yet oddly familiar, seeming to come from directly above her, yet so low it might have come from anywhere in the house over whatever distance to eventually reach her here in her coffin.

A rumble. Something trembling. Yet she felt no vibration.

She pressed her ear to the rough wood.

Continuous, almost musical.

She listened. And when finally she identified the sound she fell back into the first true sleep of the morning. Her body and mind finally settling in, attempting to replenish themselves after a day in which both had burned to exhaustion.

Until well after dawn the cat remained lying just above her heart atop the Long Box.

And for most of that time continued purring.

SEVEN

3:30 P.M.

At least she was drinking and eating a little. American cheese on white bread. Hunger kicking in, jarring loose the survival systems. At least she wasn't going to die on them.

Like the other one.

Stephen had her tied to the chair, just blindfolded this time so she could eat, not inside the headbox. He said it was time Kath made her presence known, time for her to begin. So that was what she was doing.

Light from the single bare 100-watt bulb that dangled from the ceiling made weird ugly shadows in the corners as though things were crouching there, hemming them in. She would never get to like this room. No matter how much time she spent here.

She took the empty plate and patted Sara's hand.

"Good," she said. She walked to the back of the room and put the plate on the worktable and sat down in the director's chair in front of her.

"Who are you?" Sara said. "Why am I here?" The voice wasn't strong but it wasn't exactly meek either.

"The Organization wants you here. Same as me."

"You?"

"That's right."

She watched the woman consider it.

"I don't believe you. I don't believe in any Organization."

She laughed and bent over and took her hand in both of hers, a little surprised when she didn't try to pull away. Maybe this was going to be easier than she'd thought.

It was still too early to tell.

"You'd better believe. Look, I'm not supposed to be saying we know this but I will. Your father's a retired high school principal. I forget what year he retired. Your mother never worked again after you were born. Strictly a homemaker from then on. She took care of you and your sister Linda who lives in Hanover, New Hampshire. She's forty-three and single and works as a nurse on the pediatrics ward in the hospital there. You have a good friend named Annie Graham who lives in Harrison, New York, not far from where Greg lives. Greg runs a travel agency in Rye with his wife, Diane. They have a son, Alan I think his name is, who's ten. We know your teaching schedule at Winthrop and we know all your students' names and addresses. They're upstairs on the kitchen table. Want me to go get them?"

She saw that Sara was crying softly, could tell by the way she was breathing. Scared crying.

"I don't understand," she said. And now the voice *was* small.

Kath gently squeezed her hand.

"You will. It'll take a little while but trust me, you will."

"He said something about a baby."

"There's plenty of time to talk about that. Just remember that the Organization's been watching you real close and for a very long time. Same thing with us, even though we're a part of it. They're watching us too, see, not just you. They want to find out how this goes. It's important. Believe me, Sara, I know exactly what you're feeling. I felt the same way once. I really did. It'll pass. You just have to give it time."

"Why do I have to be naked? Why did he beat me?"

She withdrew her hands.

"It's the way the Organization wants it to be. I already told you. You've got to go with whatever they want from you. Really, truly submit. With all your heart and soul. Just like I did. Then nobody else will get hurt. Nobody. Not even you anymore."

"But I don't . . ."

She got up. "We'll talk again soon, I promise. But right now I've got a billion things to do. The place is a goddamn mess. So you just sit there awhile and think about what I said. Think real hard."

"I don't . . . I don't even know your name."

She almost laughed. "Don't worry. There's time for that too. Think of it as being on a need-to-know basis. Like in the movies, right?"

She picked up the plate and flicked the wall switch and left her there in darkness thinking, *first step taken*. Stephen will be pleased.

It was important to please him.

EIGHT

The headbox seemed to have gotten smaller. That was impossible she knew but the damp darkness seemed more enclosing than before. The musty-carpet smell thicker. She tried to move her head as though movement could clear the air, circulate the air inside but she could only move it slightly, half an inch or so in either direction because the back was latched to the X-frame. She was spread-eagled on the X-frame. Facing outward to whatever, whoever was out there.

She had been here about half an hour now. That was what she guessed. Guessing the time was her one form of recreation. It held no rewards because she never knew if she was right or wrong. But it was better than thinking.

Images kept skittering like night-crabs across a moonless beach.

Rushing to the plane that day, late as was usual in those days after Danny died, so late leaving her parents' winter home in Sarasota that she almost missed the flight, a packed Freddy Laker flight where you had to seat yourself, leaning over a man in an aisle seat way in

the back, breathless, saying to him is this seat taken?
and the man who was Greg Glover she learned after two
vodka tonics to sooth her nerves, the man then taking
off his sunglasses and smiling saying no, it's all yours.

The frozen ice. The hole in the frozen ice so small she
could barely believe he'd slipped through. The surface of
the ice for yards and yards around. Searching the pale
bright face of it for a hand, a boot, a glimpse of clothing.

She and Annie little girls, kissing each other goodbye
at her dad's car because Annie went to Catholic school
and Catholic school started earlier than public school
did and it was the end of the summer so Annie had to
go back, leave Rockport and Sara who wouldn't see her
now for another whole two weeks. Both of them crying
the innocent tears of little girls who are wholly in love
with one another and unashamed.

The ice. The face she had never found but had imag-
ined countless times pressed up to the ice from beneath.
Cold ice and drifting water.

All these memories. Good and tender. Bad and
worse. Leveled somehow onto the same plane now.
Each a heavy weight upon her heart as heavy as the
headbox on her shoulders. Racing unbidden through
her consciousness to torment her.

It was better to guess the time. How long she had
been in this or that position. The exact time of day. The
hour, the minute, the creeping passage of seconds.

The only game she herself had devised and not them.

She flinched when he touched her.

He smiled and mentally noted it for later. Flinching

was grounds for punishment. Of course she didn't know that yet but she would.

He strapped the leather belt around her waist and buckled it. From the belt depended half a dozen wide silver rings but he wouldn't be needing them just now. He adjusted the belt so that the second, vertical buckle was in the center of her back and the second leather beltstrap hung directly between her legs in front. He opened the jar of Vaseline and lightly greased the thick four-inch leather dildo in the center of the belt. Opened her up and greased her too. She tried to squirm away from his fingers inside her but there wasn't far she could go on the X-frame.

Another breach of conduct duly noted.

He held her open and inserted the dildo and even with the Vaseline she was dry and tight but by moving it back and forth, in and out he got it into her up to the hilt and then ran the strap up through the cheeks of her ass and through the second buckle and tightened it firmly and buckled it off.

He could hear her faintly squealing inside the box.

He stood back and watched the roll of her hips, she was trying to scrape the thing off against the X-frame but both belts were buckled up tight, they were there for the duration, the belts were going nowhere.

For as long as he wanted.

To remind her exactly who was who in this relationship of theirs.

He walked over to his worktable and opened a drawer and took out the Polaroid camera.

* * *

All she could think of from then on was this thing inside her.

This lifeless *thing* fucking her. This constant violation.

She couldn't begin to guess how many minutes, how many hours it stayed there.

NINE

The two of them stood behind her as he lifted off the headbox and tied the black scarf over her eyes. Kath could see the raw spots where the box had rested on her collarbones. She wondered how the harness and dildo felt. It was new. He'd never made her wear one. She felt a twinge of something that was almost like jealousy but of course it wasn't that because jealousy in this case would be ridiculous. They were probably damned uncomfortable. She watched him gag her.

They moved around in front of her, Kath following behind, giving him space. Knowing he'd need it.

"Here's the story," Stephen said. "The rules are that I do anything I want with you and you don't flinch, you don't pull away. You don't resist in any way whatsoever. You understand me? Even when I put my fingers inside you like I did before. All I was doing was opening you up, lubricating you so it wouldn't hurt so much. And you try to pull away. *A* that's stupid and *B* it breaks the rules. So I guess you can figure what comes next. Sorry."

The whip had eight long leather tongues, each tongue ending in a twisted ball.

She had felt it on her own body. An evil old acquaintance. The tongues stung you, raised instant welts if he whipped you hard enough. The balls bruised you, punched at you like tiny fists. Which was worse she couldn't say.

She watched him drag the whip up sidearm from the concrete floor and slap her heavily across the breasts, first one breast and then the other, over and over, *slap, slap*, his arm like a metronome. Regular and more brutal she knew precisely because of the regularity, red streaks appearing instantly on Sara's pale flesh, she wasn't a topless sunbather like Kath was, she was probably too modest, blotching as he crisscrossed them with new strokes and she knew that the woman would welt up soon and that if he continued long enough the welts would bleed. She heard the woman screaming inside the gag, saw the muscles of her face pinch tight with pain, the body writhing and shocked by each successive blow and trying with no hope whatsoever to avoid them, every blow aimed at her breasts, each and every one with no relief except that he was moving from from one breast to the other, *not much there*, breasts being a kind of thing of his, a kind of fixation with him like having babies was a fixation with him and maybe they were connected, they probably were. He liked to suck her own breasts and bite them especially the nipples, he was like a baby himself sometimes always wanting mama's titty and she knew how this felt, she knew exactly how Sara felt under the whip. She'd been there. She could feel it in her own breasts, tingling.

She figured it must be sympathy.

TEN

They'd let her use the bedpan but now she was back on the rack again. Mercifully, her hands were only tied behind her to the center of the X-frame instead of overhead. At least her fingers weren't going numb. When her legs got to trembling too much she could kneel for a moment on the concrete floor but in that position her forearms slipped down and spread apart painfully over the lower V-shape of the frame and it was too much to take for very long. Still it provided some relief.

Whatever he'd used on her breasts had taken out most of the sting. She felt a kind of throbbing heat there and a raw spot in the center of her right nipple. The one which for some reason had taken the most abuse.

She was blindfolded, not inside the headbox.

Another small mercy.

There was a rubber ball inside her mouth. It was affixed to a leather gag strapped across her face.

They had traded the harness and vagina plug for another one in which small dildos penetrated both her vagina and her anus. She imagined she could almost feel them touching inside her.

She was cold. Her throat was terribly dry. A taste in her mouth like fallen leaves.

Humiliation. Discomfort. Deprivation. Pain.

The Four Horsemen of her own personal Apocalypse.

Her only comfort was the cat, who had taken to her for some reason or perhaps was only curious. She would feel it now and then rubbing up against her ankles, its cool wet nose and soft haunches, and once, its calloused warm front paw-pads and the tiny sharp retracted claws on her thigh just above the knee. She imagined the cat standing on its hind legs looking up at her, though as yet she had no idea even of its color or size or the color of its eyes staring up at this strange naked human tied to a tree.

She imagined a tabby. A female. She imagined her eyes were green.

Alone in the early days following Daniel's death and her divorce she had taken a six-week-old kitten, a tabby, out of the Humane Society shelter and sardonically named her Neely after the doomed Patty Duke character in VALLEY OF THE DOLLS. The cat lived with her until her death, of cancer, only last year. The name she had given to her, that of a fictional junkie, became ironic and practically prescient and not really very funny at all because in the almost three years prior to her death the cat had come down with diabetes and Sara had needed to give her insulin shots twice a day, into the heavy fold of skin at the back of her neck, at feeding time.

It was inconvenient as hell building her entire

schedule around the shots and running every morning to the litter box to check the blood-sugar levels in her urine but she did it gladly because nobody could comfort her the way Neely did. It was almost always at night that the sadness and loss and loneliness descended upon her and when they did the cat was magically always there, seemed to sense the yawning gulf of emptiness opening up inside her even as it grew, seemed ever alert and responsive to this alien human need. The cat was right there. Curled warm and soft in her lap or lying on her chest purring until these awful moments passed and long after if she wished, asking only a stroke or a scratch behind the ear or even just the heat of her body if Sara's soul could offer up neither of these just then. As though she knew that this was exactly her role in life, exactly what she was born for, this gentle service.

Sara found her lying in the darkness of her closet one day and the cat could barely raise her head. In the vet's office she held and stroked her and looked into the green-golden eyes as he administered the shots. One which would rocket her deep into anaesthetic sleep and the next which would kill her. She saw the head droop and fall and felt her heart break yet again.

She had not gotten another cat despite her family and friends' advice. There was too much loss for her in the world. And then she met Greg. For a long time he'd made her—if not forget—at least put aside the losses and focus on what they had together, on the present.

She couldn't imagine what he was going through.

Or her parents. Or her sister.

Her parents and sister didn't even know about the abortion—or the pregnancy for that matter. She assumed they'd know everything now once she was reported missing. Her parents were strict Catholics, especially her father, her sister lapsed the same as she was. Who would tell them? How?

She was glad that none of them could know the half of this.

She had to kneel again. The muscles in her calves were jumping.

She spread her arms as wide as she could to accommodate the V-shape and sunk slowly down. The floor was hard and cold. The wooden beams dug into her biceps and they began to ache. She tried to relax her legs, to breath easily and regularly. It helped.

He came out of nowhere.

How could he do that? The man was stealthy as a snake.

She felt his fingers pinch down hard on her left nipple, the one he'd whipped raw and then the other one, pinch hard and lift which meant he wanted her up off the floor up off her knees and she groaned behind the gag and complied and stood for him and still he pinched and twisted and it felt as though he were trying to tear them off but she knew enough not to try to squirm away, knew enough to bear it. She stood and took it from him and finally he stopped.

"Didn't say you could do that. Did I."

When the whip came down across her breasts again

she thought she would faint but she didn't, her body wouldn't give her even that much, her body was useless to her as now she felt suddenly it *always* had been, though pregnancy and childbirth and then this pregnancy too all useless and giving back nothing, even the pleasure of sex, that too useless ultimately. The body had always betrayed her. All it gave it took back and at the end of it was always pain, her breasts flooded with, engorged with pain, pain like mother's milk inside her and maybe she deserved this after all as he said she did because everything she touched either died or was destroyed. Her body, her touch, a poisonous flower torn up out of a sour earth.

What do you think, daddy? Do I deserve this? Your little girl?

She didn't know what he'd say. He'd maybe say she did.

When it was finished he allowed her to sink to her knees, said she had permission to do so now and she should always ask in the future and she hung there not even aware of the wood bruising into her biceps and wept behind the blindfold. Exactly what she was weeping for she wasn't sure but she knew it wasn't just the pain.

A strange thought occurred to her which wasn't exactly a Catholic thought but which certainly partook of that.

Sin begins with a repugnance for the flesh.

She stared into her soul and saw herself a sinner.

ELEVEN

11:45 P.M.

They sat in the dark watching the latest Jackie Chan movie on Cinemax. He was thinking how easy these kinds of movies were, the plots so familiar you didn't have to follow them. You could think about other things like how he was going to have to start work on restoring Ruth Chandler's hutch tomorrow and what he was going to do with Sara Foster once Kath went back to work Monday. You could think about this stuff and plan things until the next fistfight started and then go back to it once the fight was over. He decided that Monday she'd spend the day inside the Long Box. Total dark. All day long. Every day he'd soften her.

He was thinking that sitting in the flickering shadows finishing the leftover stuffing from last night's chicken when the doorbell rang.

So who the fuck was that? At this time of night. He'd made a point of not cultivating the neighbors. He looked at Kath on the sofa and saw she was thinking the same thing he was—*cops, we're fucked*—and felt a moment of utter panic, wondering if he shouldn't get his ass out the back door double-quick.

Then he thought *no way, I got this covered*.

It couldn't be.

He put his fork down on the plate and set it on the end table and turned on the lamp beside it and got out of the chair. Jackie Chan was getting punched out by some black guy. It wouldn't last. Chan would break his nigger ass. At the door he put on the porch light and looked out the window.

McCann. Jesus, McCann of all people. He didn't need this. Not today.

But he couldn't very well play at *nobody home* either. Not with the TV blaring.

He opened the door.

"Stephen."

"Mr. McCann. How are you?"

"Fine. I know it's late. May I come in a moment?"

"We were just about ready to go to bed, actually."

"Only a moment. Something's been on my mind. It won't take long. I promise."

The smile was unctuous as usual. There was something about the little bearded bald man that always revolted him. McCann was a lifelong bachelor. Probably a faggot. Their interests had led them into the same circles but for very different reasons. Stephen didn't have to like him.

"I guess. Where's your car?"

"In the shop, I'm afraid. I walked over."

McCann lived about two miles away, practically into the next township. What the fuck was *this* all about?

He decided he'd better find out.

McCann stepped into the room and Stephen ges-tired toward the chair. He turned off the volume on Jackie Chan. Chan and the black guy fought on in silence.

"Thanks." McCann sat down and sighed.

"Can I get you a beer or something?"

"If sinners entice thee, consent thee not."

He chuckled. Actually chuckled. The asshole.

"Thank you. That would be most welcome."

"Kath? You?"

"No thanks."

He walked into the kitchen and got two beers and opened them and when he returned to the living room both Kath and McCann were watching the silent screen. Both of them looking distinctly uncomfortable. McCann took his Bud and drank. Stephen sat down beside Kath and did the same.

"So. What can we do for you?"

"I may as well say this right out. I have to know, Stephen. It's been bothering me. Where is she? *Who* is she?"

"What are you talking about?"

"The woman. In front of the clinic yesterday. I wasn't supposed to be there, you see. The New York Christians' Aid Coalition called some of us from my group at the very last minute. A number of their people had cancelled. Elsie Little and I were the only ones who were free yesterday. But I saw you. You pulled her into your station wagon."

"I don't know what you're talking about."

He sighed. "I *saw* you, Stephen. If for no other reason than for the movement's sake I need to know exactly what's going on here. Remember, *he that loveth lies loveth not the Lord.*"

"You've got me mixed up with somebody else, Charles."

He smiled. "You and Katherine both? That's hardly likely. I saw both of you. I even recognized your car. Trust me, Stephen, please. This is just between the three of us. Elsie didn't notice you and I haven't said a thing to her. You can trust me."

He'd sooner trust a water snake.

He wanted to strangle the little man. But McCann was scaring him too.

They'd planned it to be in a whole other State. The biggest city in the world for god's sake. A place they'd picketed only once before. Nobody they knew was supposed to be anywhere *near* there.

He pulled heavily from the bottle.

"She's going to have a baby," Kath said.

"What?"

"Jesus, Kath!"

"She's going to have a baby. She's three months pregnant. I can't have one and she can. And with Stephen's record we can't adopt. So she's going to have *our baby*. Okay? You satisfied?"

"But . . ."

"She was going to *abort* it, Mr. McCann. Remember the first commandment? *Thou shalt not kill?* Remember what this is all about? We are saving the *life* of this baby!"

McCann stared at her and sipped his beer. Stephen was alternately furiously with her and relieved. The ball was in his court now.

It was unlike her to be so passionate.

Maybe she disliked the little toad as much as he did.

"Do me a favor, Kath. Get me another beer, will you?"

She got off the couch without a word. Just as glad to be out of it. McCann's eyes followed her and then settled back on his.

"You really expect to *do* this?"

"Yes."

"But you can't just . . . kidnap somebody. What about consent?"

"We'll get her consent."

"How in the world will you do that?"

"That'll have to be our business, I'm afraid."

He shook his head. "Not the Lord's business, I think."

"Maybe yes, maybe no. Is abortion the Lord's business?"

"We're trying to end that."

"I know. In our way so are we. Here's one kid who's not going to get sucked out of his mother's womb like some dustball off a living room floor."

"But the *real* mother . . ."

Kath handed him the second beer and sat down beside him again.

"To hell with the real mother. She was going to kill it."

"*It?*"

"The baby. Him. Her. Whatever."

The man glared at him. Stood up.

"All right, let's *see* her, then. Let's see this . . . this *brood mare* of yours!"

"I gotta tell you. I don't like your tone, McCann."

"I don't like your choice of words, either. A child is

not an *it*. Motherhood is a blessed state and you cannot simply lift your choice of mothers off the street. Where is she? In the basement? That's where *I'd* keep *my* prisoners."

The man was actually trembling with anger. *The self-righteous little bastard*. He shook his finger at both of them and headed for the basement door.

"Isaiah 7:3. *Amend your ways and doings, all ye whores and defilers!*"

Something inside him gave a desperate lurch and he was up off the couch reaching for the second bottle and suddenly he was armed and fucking dangerous, one of the bottles dripping with cool sweat, he had them by the neck and he swung the empty down over the man's ear, felt the impact and heard and watched it shatter and then he was looking down at his hand again, the suddenly truncated neck of the bottle sticking jagged and deep into the pad of flesh between thumb and forefinger. He looked up and saw the man turn trying to say something and swung the other bottle, the one that was almost full, directly into his face.

It was a kind of magic he thought what a simple glass bottle could do. One moment the face was full of fury and indignation and the next full of surprise and pain because the second bottle had shattered too but this time full across his mouth, a huge shard of brown glass pushed through the upper lip and out his cheek, foam and blood mingling in a bright pink slime riding down his chin.

Dimly he could hear Kath scream and the little man

roaring deep and anguished but his brain was roaring even louder saying, *finish it, you got to finish it!* even as McCann reached for him. He pivoted and half-dived and half-fell over to the end table, the plate that had held last night's stuffing clattering to the floor, the fork which was his target in his hand and he reached up off the floor as McCann lunged for him, McCann unaccountably still wanting to fight and shoved it deep into the man's neck and twisted, twisted fast back and forth inside him, sinking it deeper until the hands closed over his own and tore them away with an unexpected force and tore the fork from his throat and sent it sailing across the room.

The man's growl gurgled in his throat, the throat pulsing blood through his clasped hands like Stephen's own first pulsing orgasm when he was a boy, blood rolling off the pierced cheek and spraying from his throat over the throw-rug in front of the TV and over the TV screen where Jackie Chan fought on as he staggered to one knee and *finish it finish it* still wailed in his ears so he tore the shard of glass out of the palm of his hand and ripped the plug from the heavy brass standing lamp beside the couch and grabbed it by the neck and brought the base of it across McCann's face as hard as he could hitting him with five solid pounds of brass, a sound like metal striking a bowling ball, knocked him sideways to the floor, blood spraying the wall and the mirror over the fireplace in the wide arc of his fall. He stood over him and brought the base down on his head, he didn't know how many times, over and over until the sickening *thuds* turned gradually softer, until the body stopped twitching and the flow of blood grew thick and languid as a mudslide. Until he could barely even lift the thing any more and collapsed to his knees beside him.

He realized he was crying. He looked at the mangled head.

He got up on quivering legs and rushed to the sink and delivered himself up of cold bread stuffing and meat loaf dinner.

He turned on the tap and the switch on the disposal unit and rinsed the stuff away and rinsed the gash between thumb and forefinger. With the other hand he splashed his face. The cold water seemed to revive him. The cut continued to seep blood in regular pulses so he wrapped it with a clean dish towel out of the drawer and used his teeth and his good hand to tie it tight.

Kath was still making tiny high-pitched keening sounds. Rocking back and forth on the couch. Staring at the ceiling. Her face shiny with tears.

It seemed as though he saw blood everywhere.

Gotta clean up, he thought.

Gotta shake her out of this and clean up and get rid of McCann in the back where the girl was and the thought occurred to him then that maybe he could *use* this.

Maybe this was even *good*.

But first he wanted towels. First things first.

To wrap that head.

* * *

Downstairs in the long box she dimly heard a voice she didn't recognize raised loudly in anger and at first she thought it was the television turned up high, then that maybe *just maybe* it was someone who had come for her. The police. Someone. The thought made her heart race. Then moments later she heard a struggle. Feet pounding heavy across the floor and glass breaking and then more and more pounding and she thought *yes! get them! get the fucking sons of bitches! and then please please hurry*.

And then heard only silence.

She pounded on the box. Kicked at it. Shouted, screamed.

No one came.

She lay there for god knew how long, listening to her own breathing. She heard running water through the pipes *on-off on-off* and the occasional heavy footfall and that was all.

Hope seeped away like water down the pipes and left her numb and empty.

The pain returned too.

Her breasts mostly. But also her back and shoulders and her ass pressed against the cold hard wood. There was no way to get comfortable inside the box, no way to fully relax her aching muscles. Inside the box, sleep came with a hammer in its hand or else it didn't arrive at all.

Once again her life reduced itself to waiting.

How many days? One? Two? Three now?

When she finally heard footsteps cross the room moving in her direction she knew that they belonged to him and not to some deliverer. At best he was coming to feed her or ask if she needed the bedpan. At worst she'd be beaten again for some unknowable infraction or put inside the headbox. She was resigned to all of it.

· She heard his fingers on the latch and his voice telling her to put on the blindfold and she did and then she was sliding out into the room again.

"Stand up."

She was always a little dizzy after being inside. She stood slowly and carefully, using her hands on the top of it to support her for a moment until she felt sufficiently steady.

"Put this on."

She felt fabric, cotton, press lightly against her stomach and she reached for it with both hands and hugged it to her, smelled the clean fresh scent of it. She unfolded it, turned it.

"The other way. You got it wrong. That's the back."

She turned it again.

Clothes! He was giving her clothes!

A dress!

She pulled it on over her head and winced as it slid across her breasts but that was nothing to the sensation of being clothed again. It was probably a little baggy, a little bit big for her she thought and yes, it was, she knew as she began to button it. But the light thin material felt wonderful.

A short-sleeve dress. She almost felt human again.

"These too. They're yours."

He handed her her shoes. The flats she'd worn to the

clinic. Their familiarity tore at her as though they were of another life entirely, relics of some dimly familiar well-loved past. She leaned back against the box and slipped them on.

"Thank you," she said.

"You're welcome. Put your hands behind your back."

He snapped the manacles together.

"Come with me."

He took her arm, firmly and not gently, and suddenly she was frightened again. But she did as he said and walked with him. There was nothing else she could do.

"Where are we going?"

"You don't question me, remember? You'll see."

Maybe this is the end, she thought. Maybe they're going to do it now.

End me.

Kill me. Or let me go.

No. Not possible.

"Careful. There are stairs here."

He led her up slowly. She counted the steps, trying to calm herself, trying to interrupt the circle of excitement and fear which looped into each other inside her. Neither excitement nor fear would do her any good. She counted sixteen wooden steps. They came to a carpeted landing. Fresh air swept cool around her ankles and she thought they must be standing by the back door, that it must be off to her left. Then he turned her to the right and moved her up yet another, slightly higher step and she was standing on a wood floor. This must be the kitchen or dining room area, she thought. She smelled faint cooking-smells, hamburger or something, almost overwhelmed by cleaning-smells, ammonia, bleach, and something like Windex or Fantasik.

Simple, comfortable, familiar smells. Not the damp musty basement. They nearly brought her to tears.

"Okay, slow now."

He moved her a half-turn to the right and walked her fourteen steps straight ahead over a wood floor and stopped, took her by the shoulders and turned her around.

"Sit."

She bent her knees and reached down behind her with her hands until she found the base of a narrow wooden chair topped by a thinly stuffed cushion and sat down.

"Okay, now listen to me. I'm only going to say this once."

He was either kneeling beside her or sitting, she couldn't say which, but he was very close. His voice was soft but there was something excited about it too. A kind of heightened nervous quality. It scared her. She wanted him stable. As stable as possible.

"You heard something up here awhile ago, didn't you."

She almost said no. Then thought it was probably not wise to lie to him. She nodded.

"I thought so. What did it sound like to you?"

"Argument. A fight, maybe."

"Very good. I'm going to show you something in a little while that will probably upset you. It's all right to be upset. It's natural. But I want you to know what happened before I show it to you. Two men just left here. These two men were members of the Organization. Friends of mine. They were with a third man, Victor, who I also know very well. But Victor was a traitor. There's no other way to put it. He knew things. And we found out he was talking to the police. We have people inside there too obviously. He hadn't said anything too specific to them yet, he was waiting for their bribe money to come through. But we knew he was talking or about to talk. And he didn't know we knew.

"So what we set up was this. They all come over here for a friendly visit, a drink, some conversation, the usual. Then we confront Victor with what we know. He tries to deny it but we've got all the dates and times and people. We know which cops he's talking to. He finally admits it. He's very upset, very contrite. Says he must have been crazy, out of his mind. We agree with him there. Now what I want to show you is by way of instruction. I get the feeling you don't completely believe us about the Organization but maybe after you see this you'll think again."

He stepped behind her.

And lifted off the blindfold.

"*Victor*," he said.

Light flung itself at her eyes like swarms of stinging insects. For a moment she could see practically nothing, then saw she was in a living room. Saw chairs, a fireplace, a television set, a dusty hardwood floor.

And in the center of the floor the shape of a man. A

small man. Wrapped in heavy-duty black plastic bags tied with loops of twine.

She felt the meagre contents of her stomach rise.

"This is what happens when you fuck with the Organization, Sara. *You die*. It's that simple. Turn and look at me."

She did, fearfully, knowing the stakes were being raised yet again by him allowing her to see him. She saw a dark-haired, almost handsome man of medium build standing there in a sweatshirt and old jeans. Slim, hairline receding a little, nose a little too sharp, but with eyes that were wide and dark and actually beautiful—*how could they* be *that?*—a good strong chin and full, sensual lips. He was gazing at her directly. Not smiling.

And she had the oddest feeling that she knew him from somewhere, had seen him somewhere before. That he was not entirely a stranger.

She said nothing.

She wondered where the woman was. If she would be familiar too.

"You think we're still fooling you, don't you. That Victor's some mannikin or something."

He was right. After the initial shock that was the first thought that came to her. The mind simply rebelled. She couldn't be sitting in a room with a murdered man lying on the floor in front of her. It just wasn't possible.

Do you really know the limits of the possible? she thought. *In this place? Do you?*

"Get up. Go over and touch it. Here."

He reached around and unfastened the manacles. It

occurred to her that this was far and away the most freedom she'd had since the moment they took her.

She could run for the door.

Why don't you, then?

Because the door is probably locked and even if it wasn't he'd catch her easily. That's why.

She stood, already dreading what she was going to find. If this thing on the floor were a mannikin why would he call his own bluff?

She walked over and knelt and for a moment couldn't bring herself to touch it but he was standing behind her staring, she felt his stare like a harsh command so she reached out and gave a push to the center of the thing and it was the weight of a man all right, no mannikin ever felt so heavy nor the flesh beneath the bags so giving and it couldn't be a living man pretending either because one of the bags was tied off tight at the neck and there was no way in the world he'd be able to breathe inside.

She was kneeling next to a dead man. A man he'd just admitted killing.

And they would do it to her, he said, if she defied him.

If he'd raised the stakes by showing her his face he'd raised them infinitely higher by showing her this. There was no way in hell he could let her live now unless she either escaped or submitted wholly to him and to this Organization he kept talking about.

Whether the Organization even existed or not really didn't matter. Though she now thought that maybe it did. Was it so far-fetched after all? Cults existed. White slavery existed. Neo-nazis existed. In the end it didn't matter. Even if it was all in his mind, even if he was crazy, what mattered was his power over her. The power to extend her life or take it on a whim.

The back door opened and she saw the woman standing there on the landing in cutoff jeans and a baggy tee shirt. An ordinary-looking woman, in her early forties she guessed like the man appeared to be, neither homely nor pretty, braless, with long slim legs. She looked directly at Sara for a moment and then went into the kitchen. Turned on the water and began to wash her hands.

"It's ready," she said.

"Good. Sara?"

She turned to look at him. She heard the water go off in the kitchen and a paper towel ripped off the roll, sandals crossing the floor toward them and knew the woman was in the room with them but she didn't take her eyes off him for an instant.

"You're going to help us bury Victor. By doing so you'll be helping us accomplish two important things. One, it'll look very good for you in the eyes of the Organization. In fact you're doing it at their direct request. Two . . . well, call it a kind of bonding factor. As far as the police go, should you ever decide you need to report this, you'll be an accomplice to murder.

"Oh, I know what you're thinking. You're doing this under duress. So if you tell the police *that*, no problem. But the Organization has that covered too. We've done this before, you know. We've had practice. Once we finish with Victor here I'm going to sit you down with some pens and paper and you're going to write us a few letters, post-dated. They'll be friendly letters—I'll tell you what to say, don't worry—as though Kath and you and I are old buddies from way back. You'll write, among other things, about how much trouble you're having actually going through with the abortion. As though we've been advising you not to have one all along and you're slowly coming around to seeing things from our point of view. Know what I mean? Then in the final letter you'll ask us, if you *do* decide to keep the baby, if it's okay for you come out here to stay awhile. Y'see? You get the idea? It'll look like you're here because you *want* to be. Period."

"What about the envelopes?"

She almost bit her tongue for saying it. She knew damn well it was dangerous. But she had to try to shake him somehow. She felt trapped and resentful. She had to let him know that without defying him.

"Excuse me?"

"The envelopes. They'd be postmarked. Dated. You can't fake the postmarks."

He smiled. "Who keeps envelopes, Sara? You throw 'em in the garbage. But nobody'd think twice about people who keep letters from an old friend. Here's the finish. Finally, what we'll do is, we'll give you back your address book for a minute or two. Let you enter our names in. Like we've been in there all along. We figure that about covers it. Don't you?"

She supposed it did in some twisted way. Would the police really believe this? They might.

In any case she nodded.

"Good." He stood. "Let's get going. Kath's already dug the hole for us. You get the honor of covering him up. Kath, you and Sara get his legs."

She hesitated, warring inside.

I can't do this.

Yes you can. You've got to.

You can't just take a man out into the backyard and bury him. This isn't happening.

Want to bet?

"I'd do it if I were you," the woman said.

Kath. Her name's Kath. One more revelation. Her voice sounded cold, distant. Almost rehearsed.

"Your father plays golf at the Fairview Country Club," she said. "Plays mostly Saturdays. Do you know how easy it is to shoot a man on a fairway? With a high-powered rifle? Remember what we told you, Sara. You're not in this alone. You're responsible for and to a lot of other people.

She paused to let this sink in. It did.

"So. You want the right leg or the left?"

And then the weight of the man, the stiffness of his body, the night air cool through the thin cotton dress and her own unwashed smell rising off her as they carried and dragged his body across the lawn, dew at her ankles, the one behind her the only house visible, carried him back through the line of evergreen trees and into scrubby woods to a crude four-foot hole in the ground and dumped him in, the feel of the shovel in her hands which she might have used to crack their skulls but for the baseball bat he held tapping against his leg, the blisters rising hot and sore along her thumb and forefinger, the sound of earth falling first on black plastic and then more softly upon itself, the smell of damp heavy earth, of mold and decay seeming to enfold her, thinking I'm burying myself here, it's me, it's me I'm burying.

It's me.

THE THIRD DAY

TWELVE

June 10, 1998
11:45 P.M.

The headbox again. The still stifling air. The silence.

She'd been standing alone for what must have been hours. Her belly pressed to the X of the crossbeams, arms and legs manacled, legs spread wide apart and arms low across the center of the X to insure circulation. It was as though she were hugging the thing. Not punishment, he said, just convenience this time. They were going out to a movie. They were going out for a pizza. They needed to get out of the house for a while. As though it were the most ordinary thing in the world just to leave her here.

The day after she'd buried a man.

The day after they had killed him.

Before he left he'd slipped the bedpan between her legs and she'd used it a while ago, pissed into the silence, unable in the deep thick quiet of the box even to know if she'd hit or missed her target, only knowing that some of it had run down her leg and still felt sticky and uncomfortable along her thigh, a trail of her own self-disgust because she could do nothing to stop this new humiliation nor any other. It was a wonder to her that a human being could turn so powerless all in the course of a few days' time. Not even days. In moments.

Their faces haunted her, inhabiting the dark inside the box like pale flickering holograms. The woman's face so empty of feeling, of any recognizable emotion at all as though this were nothing to her. Routine. Another day in the life. His face nervous and unsettled— reading lust, greed, power.

She had written out and signed the letters he dictated but was certain they'd fool no one who actually knew her. The language was his language, not hers. Stilted, formal. It betrayed him. It was not going to convince anybody that she was here on her own free will much less an accessory to murder.

"... *I am filled with uncertainty and doubt. A baby's life is a sacred thing, isn't it? How dare I take this step?*"

What's your problem? she thought, whoever the hell you are. Why's this so damned all-important to you? What happened? Mommy never breast-feed you?

The woman, Kath, was only along for the ride. It seemed obvious that none of this was her idea. That didn't matter, though. Because it was also obvious that she'd continue to play her part in Sara's nasty little drama. But she knew that the craziness originated with him. That if there *was* an Organization it was he who'd joined it, he who'd decided to capture her, he who dreamt up the tortures and humiliations. The woman was just a follower.

She wondered how willing a follower. Was there any weakness there? Anything she could exploit? She doubted it, but she'd watch for it nevertheless.

Watch for it. Now *there's* a bad joke, she thought.

She hadn't seen anything but the dark and the images inside her head since entering their names in her address book the night before. They'd blindfolded her, stripped her and led her down here to lie the night through in the Long Box, in her coffin. Got her up and fed her a peanut butter sandwich and tied her naked to the chair—which she realized for the first time today was bolted to the floor. Fed her again and hung her on the X-frame for however long it was going to take them to see their movie and eat their goddamn pizza.

For however long they wanted.

Her breath smelled old and stale and sour inside the box. An old person's breath.

She was growing old here.

The baby still blooming inside her.

The beautiful baby girl. The one she'd wanted to kill.

No, goddammit, that was *his* thinking. An abortion wasn't murder. An abortion was only her, Sara Foster, in the act of controlling her own body. Exercising will and choice over her own destiny. If anything *this* was closer to murder. This utter forced *loss* of control to the point where she couldn't even take a piss without fouling herself or feed herself or take a drink except when he permitted it. You could murder a personality, an identity, just as easily you could kill the body.

She wondered how long it would take for him to do

that. To make her into another little zombie like Kath who wanted only to please him and accepted whatever he did or wanted.

Even to digging graves for him.

She wondered if he could. She knew about brainwashing. She knew it was possible. But possible *for her?* That was another thing.

Resisting could mean death. Pretending was risky in the extreme. Giving in was unthinkable.

Could he really expect her to have this baby *for him?*

To live the next six months this way and then give birth to a child?

The idea was monstrous. Lunatic.

And *why?* What could he have in mind? For the baby or for her?

Zombie mother? Zombie child?

She jolted, felt hands on the headbox, undoing the clasps, the base of it chafing her collarbone again as they did so and then felt the hands lift the hook on the box off the eye on the X-frame and she sucked in damp cellar air through her mouth as he lifted the foul thing off her.

"Don't turn around. Don't speak."

He looped the blindfold over her eyes and tied it off.

"Open your mouth."

He pushed the soft rubber ball into her mouth, stretching her jaw, the taste of it bitter and dry. He tied the gag over it. Her hair caught up in the knot but she made no protest.

Whatever this is, she thought, just get it over with.

She heard soft footsteps on the stairs and heard

them cross the room and thought that would have to be Kath joining him. She heard her go the work table and put something down on it—no, two things. One that sounded like ice in a glass and another heavier, thumping to the table and then a few moments later smelled something strange in the air, something that smelled like superheated metal. Like an automobile cigarette lighter and she began to tremble even before he told her.

"I'd really rather pass on this, Sara. But it's Organization rules. A slave has got to be marked with his or her owner's personal symbol. Mostly so she can be identified if she tries to run. My symbol's a *V* so that's what you'll wear. But don't worry. I'll do it where it won't show in a bathing suit or anything, I promise. I know it'll hurt for a second but after that you'll be fine. And I honestly don't have any choice, y'know? I'm sorry. Kath?"

She heard the footsteps cross the room and the burning smell was stronger and she tensed herself knowing what was to come, that they were going to brand her like a cow, scar her, that she'd wear this awful thing the rest of her life, she'd have this to remember them by even once they were dead and buried, knowing too that it was useless to struggle, that it would only be worse for her later, god only knew how much worse and she damned them and damned her helplessness and steeled herself, telling herself not to move, it would hurt even more if she moved or if they had to do it over again god forbid so she pressed her body tight to the X-frame, the X-frame was suddenly her friend, it would help her not to move and when the burning began just to the left of the crack of her ass she screamed long and hard and high into the ball and gag and heard and smelled her own flesh burn, fine hair burning and meat.

Her body drenched itself with sudden sweat, *her body wanted to put out the fire that was huge like a thousand pinpricks everywhere, not just her ass but everywhere* and when it was done she slumped groaning in her manacles and hung limp against the X-frame and heard ice and water sloshing in a metal container and then he was pressing an ice cold cloth to the wound and some of the pain slid into the cloth and out of her, coming back fierce and hot again and again as the rag cooled until he immersed it again and pressed it to her and all the while they said nothing, silent as priests standing before an altar.

Kath double-checked her work on the bandage. There was just enough play in the square white gauze pad so that when Sara moved around inside the Long Box the tape wouldn't pull it too tight and the wound would be able to breathe. Overnight the bacitracin would do its work but the V-shaped blister probably would still suppurate for a while. She'd have to watch that. Have a look at it first thing in the morning.

No infections.

The home-made branding iron, a two-pronged fondue fork with a tooled wooden handle, lay beside the cooling hot plate on the worktable. She needed to put that away. Sara was never supposed to see what he'd used to create "his symbol." He was very good at coming up with imaginative uses for everyday household items. In his hands a meat skewer, a pizza cutter or even a dozen clothespins and some twine could transform themselves into instruments of exquisite torture, worse in a lot of ways than all the belts and whips. The fondue fork was a new one but then he was always coming up with new stuff. She'd see him sometimes just sitting in a chair staring off into space and know he was dreaming about all the possibilities. Trying them out in his mind.

Sometimes just watching him would make her shudder.

She took Sara by the shoulders and turned her toward the box and gently pushed her forward. She still wore the gag and blindfold. Her steps were small, tentative. Almost childlike.

"Okay. Stop here."

The box was open but she still needed to slide out the runnered panel. Stephen had used three-in-one oil on the wheels and runners just this morning so it slid out easily.

"Guess what?" she said. "You get a treat tonight. Three treats actually. First, no gag. You saw last night— there's nobody around anyway. Plus the walls are soundproofed."

She untied it and lifted the rubber ball out of her mouth. She never liked this part. The ball was slimy. She didn't even like the feel of it when she had to take it out of her own mouth. Much less somebody else's.

"Second, you get this. Hold out your hand."

She handed her a thin faded cotton nightgown. It used to be her mother's. Her mother was dead three years now or would be in December and she'd ransacked the house for anything that might be of use to them before they sold the property. No sense wasting. Most of what she took turned out to be less useful than she'd thought. The nightgown, for instance, had sat in mothballs along with a bunch of other stuff in a box in the attic ever since. It was much too big for her. And much too big for Sara. But it would do. After a washing it still smelled faintly of mothballs but that hardly mattered.

Thanks, ma.

"You can put it on."

She said nothing, not even a thank you, only found the neck of it and then the bottom and pulled it on over her head. Kath guessed she'd have to tell Stephen about her lack of gratitude.

"But the real treat, because of the mark and all, is you get to sleep on a mattress tonight. An air-mattress. Otherwise you'd never get any sleep, you know? Stephen pumped it up for you. See? Here, lean down and feel."

She took her arm and guided her hand.

"Nice and soft, right? You need to use the toilet or anything?"

She shook her head no.

"Okay, move over here and lie down and I'll scoot you in. Careful not to scrape the bandages or it'll hurt like a bitch. Plus I'll have to do you up all over again."

She watched her ease herself down, favoring her

231

right hip, then move her legs in along the mattress and lie slowly back, once again favoring her right side.

It still wasn't going to be an easy night, she thought. Air mattress or no air mattress. Burns hurt. And what was it that they said? you bang your elbow once, you'll probably bang it again. She'd roll over on the burn at some point for sure. None of that was her problem though and Stephen was waiting for her upstairs in the bedroom. She knew he'd want to fuck tonight. She didn't know if she could handle it if he got as energetic as he had the night before. She'd be wearing the bruises from *that* little session for days.

They *also* said that killing makes you horny.

She supposed she had the proof of that one.

" 'Night," she said and pushed the panel into the box and swung the headpiece shut and threw the lock. As she stood again she smelled her own perspiration wafting up at her.

If they were going to fuck she was definitely going to need a shower.

Sara felt it immediately down at the end of the box.

The cat lay curled at her feet.

She wondered when it had crept in and how it had avoided getting hurt by the sliding panel and thought that well, cats were very agile. She'd known that since she was a girl.

She'd learned the hard way.

Her cat Tiggy was then just a kitten. She was only five or six herself and loved him to distraction. She probably drove him crazy half the time, always wanting to pick him up and hold him, chasing him around the house trying to pet him. But he was patient with her in his catlike way and tolerated her hugs and kisses until his own enjoyment began to wear thin, at which point he'd signal that enough was enough with a little meow and more often than not she'd let him drop then and let him go his way.

Sometimes though she wouldn't, not right away and the reason was his breath. His breath was one of her guilty pleasures. His fur smelled wonderful. But in some ways his breath smelled even better. It smelled to her like the seashore. It always did, whether it was fish or chicken or meat-flavored food he'd been eating and this she found amazing. It was warm and rich and its salty tang reminded her of summers by the shore. So sometimes she'd wouldn't let him go at the first meow. Instead she'd hold onto him, nose up close to his mouth for a whiff of his breath on the *second* meow. She wouldn't let him squirm away.

And just this one time he bit her.

They were out on the back lawn sitting in the grass and she was holding him, holding him too long and probably too tightly and instead of meowing the second time as he usually did he nipped her nose instead. Not hard enough to break the skin but hard enough to hurt and make her angry, actually suddenly furious at him and when she thought about it later as an adult she realized she must have seen the bite as a kind of rejection. A rejection of her love just like her father's rejection because she was a girl and not the boy he wanted. Like her mother's merely qualified acceptance.

Like other kids' rejection because she was fat and not yet pretty.

The cat sensed her fury instantly and began to snarl and spit, a small bundle of teeth and claws and though she'd never seen him angry before and it scared her, she held him away from her and let him writhe and struggle and she *squeezed* until the cat let go with an ungodly wail of abject fear and she realized what she was doing, terrorizing a small animal, taking out her anger at *somebody* on an innocent kitten. And heartsick, attacked by sudden tears, she dropped him to the grass.

He ran. But she couldn't let it go at that.

She had to get him back. Hold him, pet him, stroke him. Reassure him that it would *never, never* happen again and let him know how sorry she was and that she loved him.

So she ran too.

There was a woods behind her house and a brook, narrow and fast-running after a rain like the one they'd had the night before and the cat ran away from her back through the grass and scrub, the cat small but incredibly fast and nimble for its size and she couldn't catch him, he kept avoiding her, she was running as fast as she could and scaring him even more she knew by chasing him but her guilt was huge and overwhelming and she couldn't stop. Not until she had him home again, until she was sure he wouldn't run away for good from the monstrous awful thing she'd done *and suddenly, there was the brook.*

The cat ran along the stones by its bank but he was

in full panic by now and he slipped and fell right in front of her eyes too far away to reach. She screamed and saw him try to scale the rock he'd fallen from but his claws could get no purchase and he began to drift downstream, his meow a piteous thing now tearing at her heart, an infant calling for its mother, the cat's eyes terrified, astonished, as he started moving fast away from her in the deep pull of the stream.

She plunged through the brush trying to get ahead of him. Trying to go faster than the stream, refusing to take her eyes off him for a second, unmindful of the branches scratching at her face or the brambles tearing at her legs but only watching as though her gaze alone would stop him from drowning. She saw him go under and come up again and claw at a rock and whirl in the current, scrabbling with his paws, trying to stay afloat and all the while his wailing in her ears and the sounds of the rushing stream and finally after an eternity it widened, slowed and she stumbled into the water and had him in her hands, Tiggy so cold and wet and fragile, she could feel his heart racing against her own chest as he clung to her for dear life and went suddenly silent, looking every which way out through the woods as though he'd never seen them before. As though the whole world were new and frightening and she couldn't even say words to comfort him she was crying so hard, she could only stroke and pet him. And then the miracle, the *absolute miracle* happened.

At the steps to their porch he started to purr.

As this cat here in the box with her was purring.

She didn't know if it was this cat or remembering

Tiggy's forgiveness that started her crying but they were the first tears she'd shed that were not in fear or pain for a very long time. She couldn't move much inside the box but she bent her knees until they pressed against the top and shifted sideways until her shoulder hit the right side and reached out in the dark and wiggled her fingers.

"Come on," she whispered. "Come on. Come here."

The cat fell silent. She was aware only of the throbbing burn and the unyielding wood and the dark until in a little while she felt the soft short silky fur beneath her fingers and felt it nuzzle and mark her with its lips and cool wet nose and the warmth of its body as it lay down to settle in against her thigh. The cat immediately began to purr again and she thought there was no better sound in the breathing world.

"There's a good girl," she murmured. "There's a good little girl. There's a girl."

And then another miracle occurred.

She smiled.

He dreamed that he sat in the basement on a folding chair with his ear pressed to her swollen belly. She was huge now, her navel protruding and he was speaking to the baby not to her. He could feel his lips move over the tight smooth flesh of her belly. She was naked, her arms and legs spread wide against the X-frame and inside her the baby was listening. Understanding each and every word but unable to answer him, not yet fully formed for speech.

That didn't matter.

He told the baby about the world, about its cruelties, its ability to slight even the most talented, the most honest, the most sincere the human race had to offer. He told it about war and killing and hypocrisy and foul tainted passion and the baby listened, understanding each and every word even if the mother didn't—couldn't—understand him at all. It was as though he were speaking a foreign language as far as the mother was concerned. That annoyed him. Then angered him. He was going to have to punish her.

He stood up and didn't recognize her at all. Who the fuck was this woman? Who did *she* think she was? The woman was smirking at him, a superior look on her face and that angered him further and he went to the worktable for a pair of pliers. He was going to work on the nipples, open them up with pliers so that when the time came the baby could feed not just on mother's milk but blood too which was richer and more nourishing and suddenly he was stepping into a huge wide open field in the middle of the night and there were stars all around above and he felt very small and very much younger and very afraid of being alone at night under such a crowded sky.

And then the pliers were gone from his hand and he was lying in his bed asleep next to Kath, something tormenting his sleep, something forgotten or left undone that was making him sweat and toss in a half-sleep, on the cusp of wakefulness, trying to remember what it was he'd omitted to do when suddenly he felt something hit the window-screen behind him and push it out from the inside, something escaping and he thought, *the cat, goddammit* and he bolted upright in his bed expecting to see exactly that, the cat escaping through the window but all he saw was the fluttering curtain, pale white lace drifting slowly, hanging in the summer air.

THREE WEEKS

THIRTEEN

On the sixth day of her captivity she recognized him. It was a gesture he made, holding his arm out, his hand palm-up toward the X-frame. Directing her there. In the gesture and in the smug self-satisfied smile she saw the man on the street in front of the clinic the day of her examination, the pink plastic foetus in his upturned hand.

She knew Kath to be the woman who'd followed them inside.

She said nothing nor did she allow her eyes to register what she saw. She was not yet a week in his basement but already she'd learned how to mask her feelings unless those feelings involved pain and terror. Those she couldn't master.

Daily over the next two weeks she was beaten on the X-frame. Sometimes blindfolded, sometimes inside the headbox. Kath had contrived a double-thick bib of old dishcloths for her to wear against the chafe of the box at her shoulderblades. The bottom layer was faded blue. The top was faded green.

Sometimes the beatings were short, lasting only a matter of minutes, *pro forma*. Seemingly almost passionless. An exercise in power and no more. He would use a belt or a light crop.

Other times they were endless. He would spend the night with her devising new ways to torment her as other men might sit in front of the television set nursing a beer. On these nights she could feel his excitement spreading like ozone through the basement air. There were occasions when she wore only the blindfold and could hear that he was masturbating. Light liquid slapping sounds followed by a groan.

Her contempt for him was matched only by her need to conceal it.

On the ninth day he seemed to realize that she could probably hear what he was doing and put rubber earplugs in her ears from then on.

There were times when every orifice in her body was plugged except her nostrils. Ears, ass, mouth, vagina.

He grew more inventive. Bound her in exotic ways. He hung her on the frame upside down and beat her until she nearly passed out from the blood rushing to her head. He held a heat lamp inches from her skin and watched her skin redden and burn and watched her twist in pain. He poked her with knives, pins, meatforks. He strangled her with his hands and when she passed out he waited and when she woke he strangled her again.

Worst by far were his rages. She'd been told to control her bodily functions but one night it simply wasn't possible, she'd been on the rack too long and there was no bedpan in front of her so she held it as long as she could and then she just let go. Her relief at so doing ended when he came at her with the studded whip. He was very good with the whip and this time he targeted one place only, the delicate flesh of her armpits and whipped them until she could feel the blood run down her sides all the way to the hip.

He called her a whore and a cunt and a bitch and a pig and a useless cow and whatever else he could think of. Not just when he was hurting her. He used the words constantly. *Conversationally*. Reminding her that he could say and do anything he pleased.

There were days she went twenty-four hours between meals. Her only drink was water. Her food consisted of greasy cheap tuna salad or American cheese sandwiches on white bread and canned vegetable soup. It never varied. She was not allowed to brush her teeth or brush her hair. She was not allowed to wash except those parts of her he had blistered or bloodied.

She began to stink.

Inside the long dark box where she stayed through most of the day she began to mark the time by marking temperatures. Mornings it was always cool. During the course of the afternoon the box would warm both from the basement temperature outside and her body *inside* and by mid-afternoon while they were still both at work she would be slick with sweat and reeking with her own thick musky smell and would stay that way until they got around to opening it. When they let her out they would leave the box open to air out. When she got in again the temperature would drop till morning and then begin to warm again.

Her daily cycle.

On the tenth day Stephen noticed the cat moving into the box while it lay open and she was on the X-frame. The cat had come to her some nights and some nights it had not. She heard him shouting at it despite the earplugs which were never very efficient anyway and then heard Kath say something to him in a loud voice and then she heard them talking. When they put her back in the box that night the cat was there. They'd allowed it to stay. She didn't know why. But she was grateful for the cat and she thought that perhaps that was the point. To *make* her grateful. Grateful to them.

But she was grateful only to the cat. To her soothing presence. To have somebody to talk to even if that somebody couldn't talk back. Grateful that the cat didn't mind sharing with her the thick sweltering air.

The cat seemed glad of her presence too. Brushing up against her ankles as she stood tied to the X-frame or walked either to there or to the chair so that a couple of times the cat almost tripped her. She didn't mind.

When he wasn't hurting her he was telling her stories or occasionally reading scripture. The readings were usually about children or husbands and wives, slaves and masters. He liked Corinthians, Ephesians, Colossians, Genesis.

"Now Sarai, Abram's wife, had borne him no children. And she had an Egyptian maidservant whose name was Hagar.

"So Sarai said to Abram, 'See now, the Lord has restrained me from bearing children. Please, go in to my

maid; perhaps I shall obtain children by her.' And Abram heeded the voice of Sarai.

"Then Sarai, Abram's wife, took Hagar her maid, the Egyptian, and gave her to her husband to be his wife. . . ."

The stories were always about the Organization.

The house, he told her, was bugged. They monitored the phone. They had known she was here from the very beginning and got daily reports on her progress.

Organization members were everywhere. The local police precinct. The legislature. The White House.

He gave her a *Daily News* article to read about the slave trade which said that in the Mideast, Europe and even in the U.S. the growing interest in S&M had lately given rise to a brisk profitable business in female flesh, women kidnapped for sale or barter to the rich and powerful with no rights or recourse to law. To be dealt with as each owner saw fit. To be tracked down and punished should they dare and then actually manage to run away. He told her that it was his father who had introduced him to the Organization and that as a young man he'd earned enough money to put himself through college by tracking down runaways.

He told her about one escapee who managed to elude the Organization long enough to actually write and publish an article about her experience. It took months but eventually they found her a second time and returned her to her owner. They pulled her fingers off one by one and then pulled off her toes. They cut out her tongue and blinded her with a soldering gun and used a stiletto to destroy her eardrums. They enlisted an Organization doctor to cut off her arms and legs without benefit of anaesthesia and then to cauterize the wounds. Finally they hung her, still alive, by her long braided hair on a hook above her master's bed where she continued to live for three days. A trophy above him writhing in agony while he slept and read.

He showed her some of her father's mail, two circulars and a phone bill, told her that they'd been brought to him by their own mailman, who was part of the Organization too, for her to see. So she'd understand just how easy it was to get to him any time they cared to.

He showed her a roster of her students' names and addresses.

On the eleventh day, a Sunday, he ordered her to suck his cock. It was the first time she'd refused him anything in several days. He tied her to the bolted-down chair, pulled off her blindfold and produced an over-and-under double-barrel shotgun. He ordered her to open her mouth and when she would not forced the shotgun into her mouth, the cold metal cutting her lips and grinding past her teeth. She had no way of knowing if it was loaded or not until he pulled the trigger.

Which he did.

He replaced the shotgun with his cock and this time she did as he said. She wondered if he'd have dared had Kath been in the room. Two nights later she assumed she had her answer when he rolled her blindfolded out of the Long Box, told her to lie right where she was, tied her hands behind her back and shortly thereafter a naked Kath descended upon her face. She suspected this was not Kath's idea because she seemed reluctant at first but eventually began to buck and moan. And then she must have said something to him about Sara's smell because she was finally allowed upstairs to take a shower, both of them standing in the bathroom looking on so she wouldn't try to squeeze her way out the window.

In the shower as she soaped her naked belly she realized she was showing.

She wondered if they noticed.

On the twentieth day she felt the baby move inside her.

The beatings continued.

For Stephen the days passed working at his shop in town or out in the garage. Gluing down veneer, repairing legs of chairs and tables, finishing and polishing old wood. He created a pine bookshelf, a nightstand, an oak desk. He was fast and efficient and charged reasonably for his work and time. He brought each job in on schedule which was a rarity these days. He was affable, friendly, listened carefully to his clients' needs and was good at what he did. No master craftsman but then this was not New York City either. He had no lack of customers.

Either he was working with wood or he was working on Sara.

He wasn't sure if it was Sara or the shop or the struggle with McCann that had given him the case of tendonitis. But the elbow was swollen into a little marble at the joint and twinged constantly. He was left-handed and now his grip was considerably weakened and the elbow hurt miserably if he used the hand too much. There were mornings he'd have a hard time digging his keys out of his pocket and an even harder time locking the door behind him. He was popping two ibuprofen every four hours and one progesterone a day, the latter on Doc Richardson's prescription. If it didn't help in two weeks, the doctor said, if the swelling didn't go down he'd have to inject a steroid directly into the tendon. It wasn't a prospect he looked forward to.

Every time he used that arm to swing the whip or drive a nail it hurt him.

He began to have fleeting headaches and strange, frequent memories of his mother's funeral.

At the service they'd set six metal folding chairs at the gravesite, one for each of her chief mourners. His father, his mother's sister June and brothers Bill and Ernie plus himself and Kath. Kath had a stomach virus that grey September day so she elected to stand behind the chairs and he to stand with her. At eighty two, with heart disease and emphysema Uncle Bill found it easier not to sit only to have to stand again so he stood too. Which left three of the six chairs empty.

His father sat in the middle. Aunt June and Uncle Ernie sat together to the far left. There was no love lost between his father and either of them. So that one chair remained open to the left of him and two remained open to the right. The minister invited any other members of the assembly to have a seat but not a soul among the twenty-five people or so attending really wished to sit with him. The mourners were there for his mother, not for him. He realized his father had not a single real friend among them and no family of his own left and thought with some amazement that he'd never seen anyone look quite so lonely.

That his father should sit unattended wasn't right, wasn't even proper and disconcerted by this, embarrassed, the minister asked again.

Again there was hesitation. Why he didn't sit with his father himself he didn't know but instead he stayed with Kath. Finally two old women Stephen had never seen in his life took pity on him or perhaps they took pity on the minister and filled the vacant seats on either side. The sixth chair remained open throughout the ceremony as though for some departed guest.

Why this memory should come back to him now so frequently puzzled him. But it came at the strangest times. When he was going for the whip. When he was emptying her bedpan those few instances Kath wasn't around to do it. When he manacled her to the X-frame. The time they allowed her upstairs for a shower. He would see his father sitting alone and stony in that folding chair.

One day over dinner he realized that he was disappointed with Sara in some ways. Or disappointed with his own responses. It seemed to him that his fantasies were never quite matched by reality when he acted on them. Her sufferings were never quite as provocative as he'd imagined, her helplessness and nudity never quite as stimulating, her submissiveness never as fulfilling. He probably needed to be more spontaneous, he thought. To plan less and *imagine* less. That way he wouldn't always be forced to match his thinking to reality.

He also recognized early on the need to escalate. At least for now.

To push his limits as well as hers. That was what the strangling was about and the heat lamp and the studded whip.

He'd promised Kath he wouldn't fuck her but he didn't say anything about her using her mouth. No promises there. Even so she'd been angry about the blowjob and he thought that telling her was probably a mistake. But for some reason he couldn't *help* but tell her. He *needed* her to know. It was part of being Kath's master as well as Sara's. So was having her sit on Sara's face. She hadn't wanted to do it. He'd had to threaten a whipping.

Escalate.

It was actually a little scary. On the twelfth day he had her on the X-frame and inside the headbox and he'd taken a Swiss Army knife off his worktable. His idea was to use the corkscrew on her clit. See what it did to her. But instead he automatically opened to the long blade. He always kept it sharp. He thought, fine, I'll use that first on her nipples and then the corkscrew on her clit but when he approached her with the knife in hand he started to shake. He started circling the areola which seemed to be darkening as the pregnancy advanced but the shaking got worse. He had to stop.

You're afraid you're going to kill her, he thought.

You really could some day, you know that? You could go too far much too soon if you let yourself.

Which made him a little afraid of her.

Not that she'd get away somehow because that was damned unlikely and besides, the Organization stories were working, he could tell. No, you're afraid of her because she might just make you want to kill her one of these days just by being *available* for the killing and that would be *very* spontaneous and very *much* an escalation, wouldn't it?

Then he thought about the baby. It would be terrible to harm the baby. She was just beginning to show.

He felt sure she'd have made a good mother.

In some ways he actually admired her. She had guts and will and stamina. The will he'd have to break, was already breaking but he wanted to let her hold onto the stamina. She'd need it for what they had in mind.

He folded the sharp blade back into the Swiss Army knife and pulled out the corkscrew and when the shaking stopped finally he went to work on her the way he'd planned to.

Kath wished she could call Gail. Her best and oldest friend. They'd met way back in nursing school and stayed friends even though these days Gail lived in the City working at Bellevue. But Stephen was always afraid of somebody dropping by unexpectedly. She wasn't going to be allowed to encourage friendships for the duration. The duration was turning into a damned long time.

It wasn't fair.

She hated the isolation.

She thought that Sara wasn't the only one imprisoned here.

Sure she had work at the hospital to get her out of the house five days a week but she didn't really have any friends among the staff there. He wouldn't let her go to any meetings or rallies either. He didn't want them to be seen, he said, till it was over. So she was stuck with the house and the basement and the television and that was it.

He'd almost completely stopped fucking her. That was another thing.

On the sixth day she drove home from work in a blinding summer rainstorm and ran directly upstairs to run a good hot shower and change out of her drenched clothes and when she came back down toweling her hair, wanting to get a Coke from the fridge, she saw that the door to the cellar was open. She felt a moment's panic thinking that somehow she'd managed to get out of the Long Box, to get free. Until she looked out the window and saw that Stephen's pickup was parked behind her own car in the driveway.

She walked downstairs and saw that he hadn't even bothered to change out of his work clothes which were just as wet as hers had been. Wet sawdust caked the legs and knees of his jeans.

He already had her out of the box and up on the X-frame and was beating her ass with a paddle. He had the paddle in one hand and his cock in the other and she turned and went upstairs. Grossed-out and furious at both of them.

She knew perfectly well why she was mad and disgusted with Stephen.

Her feelings for Sara were more complex.

On the one hand it was as though Sara were a kind of rival. He sure as hell had never run home to have sex with *her* five minutes after walking through the door.

But she was also aware that Sara was her savior too in a way. That if it weren't for Sara up there on the X-frame it would be her. And if her sex life was practically nonexistent these days so were the kinky games he always needed to play.

So why was she so mad at her? Why so disgusted?

The disgust part was easy. The dull unwashed hair. The stink of sweat and sometimes urine. She could guess that the mad part was just plain jealousy. Jealousy over the baby she carried inside and jealous that he wanted her—wanted to use her in spite of the dirtiness and the smell. But she kept coming back to the fact that it was Sara or it was her up there and why in the world would anyone in her right *mind* be jealous of the *way* he was using her because it *hurt* for god's sake. It was fucking degrading and it hurt. It confused her.

Anyone in her right mind, she thought.

Maybe she *was* crazy. She'd considered it seriously from time to time.

Maybe you'd have to be crazy to live with him.

But she'd stuck thus far. She knew she'd play it through. She'd lie to Sara and befriend her—she was turning into a world-class liar—take her side in little things like the shower and the cat, talk to her quietly and seriously about the Organization. All of it an act. See where things went. That was what she'd do.

And then the oddest thing happened.

She hadn't wanted it. Stephen had kidded, cajoled, yelled and finally threatened so that eventually she gave in and went down and shed her clothes and straddled her and at first nothing was going on. Certainly Sara wasn't cooperating. Her tongue and lips just lay there under her wet and slack and then Kath started to move, not expecting much at first but doing it all on her own with no direction from Stephen and even with no cooperation coming from below soon she thought she was going to fucking explode, she was moving back and forth and side to side and directing it all herself, total power over her body and over Sara's, wholly in command of the pace and the action until finally she found herself shuddering, quivering in the grip of the most powerful orgasm of her entire life.

She couldn't believe it.

It only made her feelings all the more complicated. That this should happen *with a woman*. When she'd never even considered having sex with a woman before. And this particular woman, their captive, Stephen's captive and now in a way that was far more real than before, her own.

The night of the fourteenth day she waited until Stephen was asleep. She took the flashlight off its hook in the kitchen and walked quietly downstairs. She sat down in the chair and let her light play across the Long Box, annoyed with herself and uncomfortable with what thoughts and feelings had drawn her here. Annoyed with Sara and with Stephen too.

She could imagine her breathing inside the box. The rise and fall of her breasts. The slow small shift inside her belly.

Could imagine the cord like driftwood to which the baby clung, tossed in a rich warm sea.

GESTATION

FOURTEEN

It was only by accident that she found the equipment.

Months had passed and by then much had changed.

She knew who they were for one thing.

Stephen and Katherine Teach. Forty-six and forty-four respectively. They'd met seven years ago on a ward at St. Vincent's Hospital in Sussex, New Jersey—she knew where she *was* now too, a small rural town hours northwest of the City—where he was a patient and she was his day-nurse. He had nearly put his eye out with a chunk of wood when his power saw hit a knot in a two-by-four. They'd dated. Married six months later.

Both were only children with no living parents. Kath was Catholic and Stephen was a Baptist though neither went to church much anymore. Stephen liked to brag that it didn't matter, he'd read the Bible six times over cover to cover including the *begats*, he was his own church. They liked action movies and comedies and Chinese food and pizza. They *dis*liked housework completely. Especially doing the dishes. As though the remains of a meal were revolting to them. They had no discernable hobbies unless you counted the anti-abortion rallies and demonstrations they could no longer go to now that Sara was with them and you counted the Organization. They read only magazines—not even the newspaper. They got their news off the TV screen. Said it was easier.

They owned a CD player and never used it. Instead they watched TV.

Katherine was barren.

That was the word they used. *Barren.*

They'd always been saddened by this. They felt that a baby would solidify the bond between them. At least Kath did.

Nowadays she rarely spoke to Stephen.

So she learned all this from Kath. Who was lonely. Who was bored. Who spoke to her a lot.

And who—for lack of a better, more hideous word— *had become her lover.*

Since that first afternoon with Kath astride her outside the Long Box she had come to her more and more frequently. Always alone. Usually at night when Stephen was asleep but sometimes during the day on lunchbreaks or on weekends when he was out of the house on some errand or other, about once a week at first and then twice a week and then nearly every night.

She seemed entranced by Sara's body. You'd have thought it were a beautiful body but it wasn't. Not anymore. At least not to Sara's thinking. The body was heavy and slow. The waist was gone, the belly huge. A ragged dark line ran from the top to the bottom of her abdomen. Her legs were swollen. Blue veins mapped the surfaces of her breasts. Her nipples leaked pale nearly colorless colostrum.

All these Kath licked and squeezed and bit. Lapped at the colostrum. Caressed the swollen belly as though caressing the baby inside it. *I'm a nurse*, she said. *I'm just going to examine you.*

Kath never did bathe or shower nearly often enough.

Her insides tasted bitter.

What Kath did to her and made her do seemed to shame her and excite her all at once. When it was over she would always want to talk. Chattering away like she was talking to some girlfriend. About her patients at the hospital or the job Stephen was working on. About the weather and her car needing a tune-up and the phone bills and the payments on the house and the movie they'd seen on HBO the night before. Whatever. Nervous talk with her eyes averted while Sara stood tied to the X-frame or more often to the chair or the sliding panel of the Long Box.

She would tell her stories of the Organization that were just as bad as Stephen's.

One day she showed her pictures. Black-and-white photos of her father watering his lawn. Of her students playing kickball on the Winthrop schoolgrounds. Of her sister stepping out of her car with a shopping bag in her arms.

Of Greg. Walking some tree-lined street in Rye between his wife and son.

She was tied to the chair.

"He's handsome," she said. "I don't blame you for wanting to make it with the guy."

"We didn't just *make it*. We were lovers."

"What about the wife and kid?"

"What about them?"

"They're a *family*. Look at them. They look happy together."

She looked at the photos again. At least he wasn't smiling.

"They weren't."

"It's still a family. Why would you want to break up a family?"

"I didn't."

"You would have. You would have sooner or later."

"I don't know about that."

"I think it's fucking selfish of you. You're better off here. It's better for everybody."

If what Kath felt was a mix of shame and excitement Sara felt only the shame. But as with Stephen she submitted. Not to do so would be murderous as well as suicidal. The photos were proof if she even needed proof by then. The Organization existed. Whether they knew it or not, everyone she loved was depending on her behavior.

Stephen had shown her a pistol one afternoon. He said it was a .45. Spun the barrel for her. Threw the safety. Pointed it at her. Clicked.

She'd already seen the shotgun. Very up close and personal.

She behaved.

And as a result the whippings and the torture became less frequent. She hardly even saw the headbox anymore. They let her out of the Long Box now for long periods at a time. Insisting that she exercise for the baby's sake. Upper body bends. Belly-crunches. Leg lifts. Diagonal curls. Her diet still consisted mainly of sandwiches but they gave her juice and and milk and herbal tea and the occasional leftover Chinese takeout or slice of pizza.

She was allowed to dress.

Faded print housecoats or shifts that even with her belly still hung loose on her frame. Kath said they'd belonged to her mother and they looked it. Cheap old ladies' clothes that were hopelessly out of style. But she was as grateful for them as she'd have been for Ralph Lauren originals. She was not allowed panties or a bra.

She still had to strip on demand.

But it was Kath these days who did most of the demanding.

After the first three months or so Stephen had changed. She could pinpoint easily exactly when the change began.

The last time she'd disobeyed him.

The first and only time she'd tried to run.

She was upstairs by then, out of the cellar a good part of every evening and weekends so she could do the housework Stephen and Kath both hated. At first she was appalled at the state of the place. A nice place basically, or it could have been. Two bedrooms, one bath, a living room, a small kitchen and dining area and an attic, built just after the end of World War II on somebody's GI Bill. But everywhere evidence of casual filth and disorder. A film of grime over everything in the bathroom, balls of hair and dust in every corner, crusted toothpaste in the sink. Dust thick on all the furniture. The drapes needed washing. The rugs needed washing. The kitchen was a greasy mess.

But she set to all of it gladly. Anything to relieve the isolation and boredom and depression of the basement. At the kitchen sink she could look out a window to the yard and the trees and squirrels and the birds pecking at the lawn and rarely even think that beyond the trees they'd buried a man. She could open the windows and let in cool fresh air.

Though she set to it carefully too. Any mistakes and she was up on the X-frame again or tied to the chair, her pregnancy be damned.

The cat seemed always at her feet.

After a while she got the house in shape and from then on it was only maintenance. Vacuuming, dusting, laundry, cleaning after meals.

The bathroom was spotless. The windows gleamed in the sun.

Kath laughed. "You're a pretty good slave," she said.

She was.

There were times during her third trimester when her back ached terribly and she felt very short of breath. She knew that the shortness of breath was her uterus expanded and pushing up against her diaphragm. She had to explain this to Stephen. Who'd get annoyed with her whenever she stopped working. She was relieved when the baby dropped lower in her abdomen and made breathing easier.

For a while she'd hated the baby. The baby was the reason for her captivity. But she'd gotten used to the notion of actually having her now. Of bringing her to term and delivering.

She'd gotten used to so much else. It wasn't hard to get used to this.

Then one sunny September day there was nobody around to watch her. Nobody.

No Kath. No Stephen.

She realized this while she was letting the cat out through the back door.

The silence. The emptiness. Looming with potential.

There was nobody in the whole damn house but her, free upstairs. Just finishing up the breakfast dishes.

Kath had driven into town to do the usual Saturday shopping.

She didn't know where Stephen was. He just wasn't there. Though his pickup was in the driveway.

She couldn't believe it. She looked around to be sure. The bedrooms, the bathroom, the cellar. Even walked upstairs to the attic. She peered out the windows front and back. Nobody there. The narrow dirt road that wound down the hill to the mailbox was empty. So was the back yard all the way to the woods. The garage door was closed. He had a shop there but if he were in it he'd have left the door open and even in broad daylight she knew a light would be on inside.

She could leave. She could do it. She could walk away.

She could run.

Her heart was pounding. What about the Organization? What would they do if she got away? She could warn everyone, couldn't she? Of course she could. Tell her mother and father and Greg and the kids' parents and get the cops to protect them. Get these two arrested. Make them pay.

For kidnapping. For murder.

The Organization had a long reach, they said. They could wait and bide their time and even if Kath and Stephen were locked up in jail they'd get her. Get all of them. That was what they said.

But how could she *not* run? How could she *not* try?

Oh, god. She couldn't.

She walked to the front door and did the simplest, most amazing thing.

She opened it.

Walked down the wooden stairs she had walked only once before in all these months and that was going up, not down them, walked them slowly and carefully because they creaked and moaned under her feet and she was looking for him side to side all the time, around the tall hedges that needed trimming, along the line of trees far off to her right and then she was on the gravel path that led through the front yard to the road and she was running, aware of her bulk and the weakness of her legs, the legs complaining of too little exercise and her breath coming hard and then heard him behind her on the gravel, turned and saw him drop the rake why hadn't she checked the sides of the house? he was out there raking the leaves for god's sake *and she stopped dead in her tracks because there was no way she was going to outrun him and stood her ground and looked at him.*

He stopped running. Walked up to her, shaking his head, brows knit tight.

Then slapped her to the ground.

"Get up," he said. "Get your ass *up!*"

He grabbed her by the arm and hauled her to her feet. Marched her back to the house, up the stairs and in. The kiss of warm sunlight disappeared behind her back like a fair-weather friend. He slammed the door. She was crying so hard she could barely see and her ear was ringing where he'd slapped her and throbbed with pain. He moved her through the house to the cellar stairs and down into the cold dark.

"You fat fucking cow! Strip! Get your ass over to the X-frame. You run from *me?*"

So furious he was spitting.

"Turn around! Spread your legs. Get your arms up."

He strapped her into the manacles.

"You run from me, you bitch? I ought to break your fucking legs. You fat sow. You cunt!"

"Please, Stephen. The baby . . ."

It was her only card.

He was pacing the cellar, the studded whip in hand, slapping it against his jeans. Screaming at her.

"*Fuck* the baby! Fuck you! You know what I ought to do? You know what I really ought to do? I ought to kill you, you little bitch. I ought to kill you right now and to hell with the baby. You try to run from me? You want to go get a cop? You want to put the cops on me? Four months you been here. Four fucking months I put up with you and your bullshit and this is what I get? You little cunt. I ought to kill you and fuck the baby, to hell with the baby, screw the fucking baby."

He threw the whip at her. The heavy knotted handle struck her in the eye. He moved swiftly to the worktable and came back with the red Swiss army knife in his hand open to the cutting blade. His eyes glittered.

"You want to fuck around? You want to call the cops on me? Well how 'bout we give 'em something. How 'bout we really give 'em something? How 'bout we do this?"

He stabbed her. The soft flesh below her left shoulder.

She felt the sudden punch of the thing and the searing burst of pain.

"How 'bout we do this?"

He shoved the knife into her inner thigh. The pain was a hammer and a snakebite. Her body slammed back against the X-frame and she screamed. Through the sudden panic she saw where he was going. The hand drew back. Pointed at her swollen abdomen.

"How 'bout we . . ."

"STEPHENNOPLEEEASETHEBABY!" she wailed.

He stopped. Stared at her.

His face went pale. He staggered once and lowered the knife and then looked away from her, looked down at the floor as though studying something there and then walked slowly over to the worktable and folded back the blade of the knife and put it carefully down. Then just stood there staring at the table. Blood was rolling down her side over her hip and down her thigh across her calf and pooling at her foot. She hung there shaking. Sobbing, watching him.

"I better clean you up," he murmured. "I better clean up the mess you made. Before Kath comes home."

Now, a month later, those were practically his last words to her.

He seemed to have lost interest.

She was damn well glad of that but worried as to why. He moped around the house, drank too much beer at night in front of the TV. Mornings Kath would let her out of the Long Box and half the time he'd be still in bed or only just getting up. She'd see the empty bottles. There were times beads of sweat would break out over his forehead. For no apparent reason. He walked with a kind of stoop. His muscle tone seemed to have gone slack. He seemed almost as depressed as she was. Kath said he was worried about money, with taxes and mortgage payments being what they were. But Sara thought it was something else.

She didn't know why she should be worried. So what if he was depressed? Why should she care? The man had almost killed her. She didn't know what it signified or why it should concern her but it did.

Her apprehension resolved itself into something infinitely worse the week before Halloween when she went up into the attic looking for a replacement bag for the vacuum cleaner. And saw what they'd stored there.

"When this is over I want to find another," he said.

They were lying in bed back to back. She guessed he couldn't sleep.

She knew what he meant and she didn't like it one bit. The baby was supposed to be the glue. The baby was supposed to be sufficient. How long did he think this was going to go on? With how many?

"Jesus, Stephen. With a *baby* in the house?"

He snorted. "The baby won't know."

"What about us? What about our lives? What about our friends? The *baby's* got to have friends and so do we."

"The baby isn't going to need any friends the first year or two. I want somebody younger this time, Kath. She's too fucking old. She doesn't do it for me. She's fucking disgusting."

He was serious for god's sake. She thought back to Shawna, the first one. She'd been younger all right. Sixteen.

Buried in back a few feet away from McCann.

He'd been playing with electricity. They hadn't known she had a bad heart.

How many?

"Stephen, I want my life back. I want to have Gail over. I want to go out to dinner and a movie sometimes. I mean, is that a lot to ask?"

"I'm talking about a year or two. Once the baby's older I'll . . . settle down."

Sure. Sure you will.

"We'll take it easy for a while. But right now, you know. I've got *needs*."

Like his needs were the most ordinary, matter-of-fact thing in the world.

"Stephen . . ."

"Look. You want it to be you again? Is that what you want?"

She did not.

But she didn't want this either.

"We're going to get caught. You know that. We try again, we're gonna get caught."

"That's paranoid. We just have to be careful, that's all. Like always."

She turned to him.

"Do you realize how close we came? With McCann? What if Elsie or somebody else had seen us and not just him? We're lucky we didn't get caught right there."

"*Un*lucky, Kath. McCann was a one-in-a-million shot for chrissake. Besides, we won't be taking her in front of some crowd at an abortion clinic. We'll be taking her off the street. Any street. It'll be completely anonymous. Just like Shawna was."

She couldn't believe he was saying this.

"Listen to yourself. Don't you get it? You fucking *killed* Shawna!"

He turned and got up on one elbow and pointed his finger at her inches from her face. Jabbing at her.

"Don't talk to me like that, Kath. You hear me? Not ever."

He stared at her a long moment and then rolled over again.

"I'm your husband. You married me better or worse. You'll do as I say."

He was sick of her. Sick of her whining and sick of her sloppy body and sloppy habits. He wondered what the hell kind of mother she was going to make. He thought that maybe he'd been wrong about this all along. Right from the start. That maybe a kid was going to be one great big pain in the ass, period.

He was even more sick of Sara Foster. Her body repulsed him. The swollen blue-veined breasts, the stretch marks, the varicose veins in the backs of her knees. Even her hair had lost its sheen. And the belly itself— the *thing* itself. She was living with a parasite inside her body for god's sake. *How could a woman do that?* He wouldn't tell Kath this but experience was the best teacher and he'd privately decided that the Movement was all wrong. It wasn't a kid in there, not yet. Once it was born it would be, sure. But for now it was nothing more than a tiny parasite feeding off her and depending on her for everything from its oxygen and food to dumping its piss and shit.

The whole damn thing was gross.

He couldn't kill her, *hell, he couldn't even play with her now the way he'd played with her before, it was ashes with her body being what it was and ashes in the face of what he really* wanted *to do because he couldn't wait to kill her.* It was the only thing left he hadn't done to the bitch when you came right down to it and he knew he'd come then which he hadn't lately, hadn't *really* come.

They'd cut and pull and tear it out of her and that'd be the end of the miserable fucking life of Sara Foster.

That in mind, he slept.

FIFTEEN

"Kath. Please. What is this?"

There in the attic.

A stainless steel cart on wheels. Sponges. Sterile pads, gauze pads. Scalpels and forceps. A box of disposable syringes. Packages of sterile drapes. An IV drip. The question was rhetorical. The need to ask it, frightening.

She knew damn well what it was.

This wasn't her first delivery.

"You're planning to do it here? In the house? You can't be."

"Of course we are." She laughed. "What did you think, we're bringing you to the hospital? You'd have the cops on us in seconds."

"No I wouldn't."

Kath patted her shoulder. "Don't shit a shitter, Sara. Now come on back downstairs. Don't worry about that stuff."

"I wouldn't say anything. I swear!"

"Right. Come on or I'm telling Stephen."

She was losing her mind. She had to be. This couldn't be happening.

"Wait. All right. Wait. These things here. What are they?"

"Clamps."

They were *huge*.

"And this?"

"A spreader."

"My god. What for?"

She shrugged. "We might have to . . . you know, a cesarean section. You use them to hold back the organs . . . stomach, whatever. The spreader's for the ribs."

"Jesus christ, Kath!"

"You got to be prepared, right? You might have complications."

"I'm not going to have any *complications!*"

Kath headed for the stairs. Sara reached out and grabbed her arm. Something she had never dared to do before. But she couldn't let it go at this.

"Listen. Listen to me. Who told you to get all this? A doctor?"

"No doctor."

"You're not even going to get me a doctor? The Organization can't spare a *doctor*?"

"We don't need a doctor. I'm a nurse, remember? Look, we've got everything here. Anesthetics, whatever. Anything you're going to need. Don't get all upset about it for chrissake. Midwives deliver babies all the time."

"Midwives don't perform *surgery*, Kath!"

"Well, neither will we. Not unless we have to."

She looked away, up to the high naked wooden beams of the ceiling.

And in that moment Sara *simply didn't believe her*.

She felt herself flush and the contents of her stomach rise.

My god, she thought. I've been such a fool. Such a terrible fool. I never saw it.

I never saw it coming.

There weren't even any stirrups. They'd never even considered *normal delivery*.

This was what they were planning— had been all along. She was their little experiment. The baby would be the fruit of that experiment. But Sara was as expendable as one of these throw-away syringes here. In fact she *had* to be expendable. They couldn't keep her captive here forever for god's sake, not even the Organization could isolate her that much. Sooner or later somebody would come around to visit. Sooner or later somebody from the outside was going to know.

Certainty washed over her. Washed her clean.

They were going to kill her.

The birthing was how.

The Organization be damned. It was time to see what she could do about that.

She was well into her seventh month.

It was time to see right now.

Should have locked the damn door, she thought. Fucking stupid not to. It was sloppy.

Stephen would be pissed. But it was Stephen's fault too.

There was nothing to do but try to repair the damages.

* * *

They sat at the dining room table over some hot herbal tea. *Grandma's Tummy Mint*. Celestial Seasonings. She supposed it was meant to be nice and reassuring. It wasn't. Outside the window the day was gray and still and dark. In a couple of weeks kids would be out trick-or-treating. She wondered if any of them would bother to come out this way.

It was Saturday. Around four. Stephen was still work- ing in the garage. She could hear the whine of his cir- cular saw.

She sat and listened and drank her tea and petted the cat curled up in what passed for her lap nowadays.

"Look," Kath was saying. "In the old days they only used cesarean when the mother was dying. Now the whole thing is to save the mother *and* the baby. What you do is, you make an incision through the skin and the wall of the abdomen. Most of the time there isn't even much of a scar. Then you open up the wall of the uterus. The incision can be transverse vertical or low vertical, transverse usually because there's less bleeding and it heals better. Then you deliver the baby and we suture you up again and that's that. I mean this is all just in case. Only if there's a problem. But it's really very simple. You don't have to worry, I know what I'm doing. I've assisted on hundreds of these."

And on how many murders? she thought.

And she realized now that she was listening to a very good and convincing liar. There was only that single slip in the attic. Otherwise Kath was practically flawless. Which called into question again all these tales all these months about the Organization.

She decided she was going to proceed as though there were none.

Another weight lifted. It was astonishing. Just like that. The Organization was suddenly . . . *gone*. Frozen out of her. Trapped in the glacier of her resolve.

She was going to live.

Where in the world did I find this *calm?* she thought. She was suddenly calm as the cat was.

She decided it was in the *knowing* that she'd found it. In the certainty. What had trapped her up to now was lack of certainty. Not knowing on a daily—even momentary—basis what they would or wouldn't do to her. These people if you could even dignify them with the word people had played on that uncertainty like a harp. *Headbox or no headbox? Beating or no beating? Upstairs in the light or downstairs in the dark?* They'd kept her off balance for months now.

Was this balance? Yes it was.

Balance was knowing and knowing was calm.

Take them one by one, she thought. And no time like the present.

Do I have it in me? Yes I do.

As certainly as I have this little girl inside me.

Greg's little girl and mine.

It was the first she'd thought of him for ages. That was balance too.

"Kath? Do you think I could have a little more tea?"

She shrugged. "Sure. You know where it is."

She lifted the cat gently off her lap and put her down on the floor thinking *yes I do, I know where* everything *is you bitch* and walked past Kath to the kitchen and ran water from the sink into the mug and put the mug into the microwave and turned it on and then opened the bottom cabinet door and took out the twelve-inch stainless steel frying pan they hardly ever used, the pan looking new as they day they'd bought it, new as the stainless steel cart upstairs and gripped it in both her hands and walked over to Kath who was hunched over her mug, who had the mug to her lips sipping Tummy Mint tea and brought the pan down as hard as she could on the crown of her head, the pan ringing like a bell, the sound true and pure and brave, Kath's face driven down into the ceramic mug and the mug to the table, the mug shattering between table, teeth, flesh and bone and flooding the surface with a liquid the color of autumn leaves.

Not a sound out of Kath as she brought the pan up and hit her again, the pan musical once more against the side of her head which suddenly sprouted glistening drops of red forming a rough half-circle across her forehead at the hairline.

She examined the base of the pan. The base was flecked with blood and a stray brown hair or two. Despite the rapid heartbeat she felt steady and powerful.

"You dead yet? Should I hit you again?"

She had the urge to giggle.

No. She'd done it right so far and Kath hadn't made a sound. Only the pan had made a sound and that one was delightful—the tolling of her freedom-bell. She could still hear Stephen's saw whining in the garage but he might stop at any time. Don't push it, she thought. You still have him to deal with.

Or do you?

Car keys, she thought. Fucking car keys. In her purse. *Where the fuck was her purse?*

The purse was on the couch in the living room.

The cat peered out at her from the hall as she crossed the living room and put the pan down on the couch and rifled through the purse. She felt the baby kick inside. The baby was urging her on.

Yes! Got 'em!

The keys jingled in her hand. *Smaller* bells of freedom.

The saw outside stopped.

She picked up the pan. The pain had stained the couch. She hadn't meant to do that but hadn't thought of it either. She walked quickly through the living room past Kath at the dining room table to the kitchen and looked out the window to the garage. He wasn't there. He wasn't cutting across the lawn and walking toward the house. She couldn't see him anywhere.

What she *could* see though was that the keys were useless. Kath's station wagon was the one sitting there in front of the garage which meant that Stephen's pickup would be directly in back of it. That meant she needed Stephen's keys, not Kath's. Stephen would have them in his pocket. And now she realized that she'd been wrong before, she *didn't* know where everything in the house was because she didn't know where they kept the goddamn spares.

They weren't in the kitchen. She'd spent a lot of time in there and would've noticed them. The bedroom? The end-table drawers in the living room?

The basement?

She wasn't going into the basement. Not ever again.

Goddammit! *there wasn't time!* There just wasn't time to go through every damn drawer in the house. The sawing had stopped. God only knew what he was doing. He was probably finishing up out there. He could walk in on her at any second.

The pan felt puny in her hand.

She needed more.

She needed to get out of there but first she needed more because she wasn't going to go strolling out like the first time only to get caught again.

The shotgun, the pistol. Where would *they* be?

The bedroom. She wasn't allowed in the bedroom and though the door was never locked she never thought to disobey and go there.

She'd damn well disobey now. She had no idea how to shoot a pistol unless you counted what you saw in the movies and what he'd shown her in the basement and even less idea how to load and fire a shotgun but she was counting on the pistol to be the simpler of the two and that probably it would be the easier of the two to find, that most people would want a pistol in the nightstand drawer by the bed in case of intruders.

She went to the phone on the kitchen wall and punched in 911 and let the receiver dangle. Maybe the police would trace the call here and maybe they wouldn't but she didn't have time to talk.

Why hadn't she done this *months* ago? *911*. Such a simple thing.

Greg. Mom and dad. The Organization.

The fucking Organization!

There isn't any.

The cat followed her down the hall.

There were two night tables in the bedroom and she didn't know who slept where or which side would be Stephen's side so she went to the nearest. In the drawer there were a dirty jumble of pads and pencils, cough drops, matches, an address book, a Vicks inhaler, an open package of Kleenex, a tin of aspirin. No gun. She walked around the bed to the other side and opened the drawer and there it was, the pearl handle and the gleaming polished silver and now at the sight of it she remembered what Stephen had done that day *exactly*. As though she'd memorized it without knowing, stored it away for just this very moment. Her finger went to the cylinder latch and she checked the chamber. The gun was loaded, not even the first chamber empty. She didn't have to search for cartridges. She threw the cylinder back into place and threw the safety, left the frying pan where it was on the bed and walked out into the hall.

All you need to do is get his keys, she thought. Put the key in the ignition and drive away. And that's the end of it. The end of all of this. You have the gun. He can't stop you. He can't hurt you at all anymore.

Just get the keys.

But when she got to the living room and turned and saw him coming through the back door, slamming the door, pausing at the landing at the top of the cellar stairs, saw the old claw hammer in his hand, saw him take in the sight of Kath slumped across the table and saw his face darken with that now-familiar blush of rage it was not the keys she wanted, not anymore.

She felt her own face twist tight into a snarl and the sudden wild pounding of her heart and she raised the gun and fired twice, the gun jumping in her hands and woodchips flying off the doorjamb and as he crouched and stepped back toward the door she fired again lower this time, the bullet slamming him back against the door and bright arterial blood spurting off his thigh and he was shouting *no no no no* which she could barely hear above the high roar in her ears, his face gone sickly, cowardly white as she stepped forward and forward again with the gun held out in front of her and realized she was roaring too, a sound the like of which she'd never heard before *twice in his presence she'd made these strange and awful sounds, the first against the X-frame* and as she closed in tighter watched him try to make himself small in the corner, shrinking away, down to his goddamn proper size, trying to crouch in the corner the snake and she took one more step until she was sure she'd get it absolutely perfectly right this time, obeying the tidal pull of her own perfect instincts in this single perfect moment and shot him in the chest and shot and shot again.

Watched him slide to the floor.

Watched him smear his filthy death across the walls.

Watched urine soak his pants and puddle up beneath him.

Saw the open mouth and the open eyes and the bright blood flowing. And felt the baby kick.

DELIVERY

SIXTEEN

New York City
November 10, 1998

"Greg."

"Hello, Sara."

They'd spoken on the phone a few times though she'd yet to see him. It had been much too hard on her to have to see him.

Now it was still hard. But she was glad to.

He looked older somehow but then so did she. The hospital's bathroom mirror had revealed that very clearly to her this morning. The face that peered back at her was drawn and pale and lines she couldn't remember seeing only yesterday spiderwebbed her forehead.

"Mother? Could you just give us a minute?"

Her mother had stayed at the hospital through-out.

Her father hadn't.

"Certainly, dear." She patted Sara's hand and got up off the chair. "Nice to see you, Greg."

"Nice to see you too, Mrs. Foster."

The door closed behind her and then they just stared at each other, smiling.

On the phone there had been too many tears. Too many regrets and apologies. He was staying on with his wife and son. He was committed to them. Of course he was. He blamed himself for not finding her, for giving up hope of *ever* finding her. He'd tried, god knows. He and her mother had harassed the police for months. Of course he had. He was a good man.

It was good to be able to smile at him now.

"You saw her?"

"She's beautiful, Sara. She looks just like you. Just like her mom."

"She really is beautiful, isn't she."

"She is."

She patted the bed. "Come sit. Talk to me."

He walked over and sat down.

"Are you all right?" she said.

"I'm all right. Question is, are you all right?"

"I'm fine. A little tired. I was only in there a little over two hours. With Daniel it was more like four. I think she wanted out. Hell, I don't blame her. But what I meant was, are you all right with . . . all this now?"

"Sure I am."

"Diane? Alan?"

"Well, like I told you, Alan was pretty upset at first. But it was more knowing about the two of us than about you being pregnant. I think he's squared away, though. I know Diane is."

"You sure?"

"She says she wants to meet you. And the baby. How would you feel about that?"

Just how civilized are we going to get? was what he was asking.

"I don't know, Greg. Give me some time. Let me think about it, okay?"

"Sure. Of course."

He sat there looking at her a moment and she watched his eyes turn sad and he reached over and took her hand, the eyes saying, *is this all right to do?* and hers saying *yes, it is* while they pooled with tears, both of them still smiling and she thought, *yes, I still love you too, always will* even before he said it.

"I still love you, Sara. Always will."

"I know."

He began to cry. She squeezed his hand.

"It wasn't such a horrible thing we did, was it?"

His voice breaking with sorrow.

"No, Greg, *no.* What we did was love one another and I don't think that was horrible at all, do you? Do you really? In your heart? And you're doing the right thing now. You know you are. Alan needs you. *Diane* needs you. And we're okay, you and I. Aren't we?"

He wiped the tears off his cheek and nodded.

"What about you?"

She laughed. "I think I'm going to be very busy for a while."

She was going back to teaching when she could. Greg knew that too.

"Yeah. I guess you are. You gonna need any help? Anything I can do, I mean?"

"That's between you and Diane. But no, not at first, anyway. I've got my mother with me and we'll be fine. Talk it over with Diane if you want to. See how involved you really want to get. Then we'll talk, you and I. Take your time. We'll see."

He nodded again and then he was silent for a while. "I hear she finally died," he said. "That bitch. Katherine."

"She never came out of the coma."

"Saves us a lot of trouble, doesn't it."

"Trouble?"

"Court and all."

"Yes. I guess it does."

"I just wish I could have . . ."

"Greg. I'm sorry but I honestly don't want to talk about it, you know? It's over for me. It should be over for you too. Am I right?"

"You're right. I just . . ."

"Greg."

He laughed and shook his head.

"You're right. I'm talking like a fool. I'd probably better go. You need to get some rest."

He squeezed her hand and leaned over and kissed her gently on the cheek and then stood beside the bed but would not release her yet, did not let go of her hand, seemed to want that one last minute holding her. She realized she wanted it too.

"Have you got a name yet?" he said.

She smiled. "I'm thinking Megan," she said. "It's Anglo-Saxon. It means *strong*."

SEVENTEEN

Her mother was asleep in the guestroom. Her baby whose name was now indeed Megan slept beside her bed in the crib. She lay staring at the ceiling trying not to remember what was impossible not to remember but thankful for the soft warm bed and the quiet apartment and all her old familiar belongings gathered around her, all of it like a comforting womb of its own from which her life could go on and spread itself unconfined, grateful too for this other familiar presence at her feet who had somehow in those months taken the sting from out the whip, the edge off the knife.

The cat sleeping beside her on the bed. The cat who now also had a name.

Ruth. *Ruthie*. From the Hebrew.

Friend.

SARAH PINBOROUGH

The quiet New England town of Tower Hill sits perched on high cliffs, removed from the outside world. At its heart lie a small college...and a very old church. There are secrets buried in Tower Hill, artifacts hidden centuries ago and long forgotten. But they are about to be unearthed....

A charismatic new priest has come to Tower Hill. A handsome new professor is teaching at the college. And a nightmare has settled over the town. A girl is found dead and mutilated—by her own hand. Another has slashed her face with scissors. Have the residents of Tower Hill all gone mad? Or has something worse...something unholy...taken over?

TOWER HILL

ISBN 13: 978-0-8439-6052-5

✂ ☐ **YES!**

Sign me up for the Leisure Horror Book Club and send my
FREE BOOKS! If I choose to stay in the club, I will pay only
$8.50* each month, a savings of $7.48!

NAME: _____

ADDRESS: _____

TELEPHONE: _____

EMAIL: _____

☐ I want to pay by credit card.

☐ VISA   ☐ MasterCard   ☐ DISCOVER

ACCOUNT #: _____

EXPIRATION DATE: _____

SIGNATURE: _____

Mail this page along with $2.00 shipping and handling to:
Leisure Horror Book Club
PO Box 6640
Wayne, PA 19087
Or fax (must include credit card information) to:
610-995-9274

You can also sign up online at **www.dorchesterpub.com**.
*Plus $2.00 for shipping. Offer open to residents of the U.S. and Canada only. Canadian
residents please call 1-800-481-9191 for pricing information.
If under 18, a parent or guardian must sign. Terms, prices and conditions subject to
change. Subscription subject to acceptance. Dorchester Publishing reserves the right to
reject any order or cancel any subscription.